# MEET ME IN THE DARKNESS

## PRAISE FOR THE BUTTERFLY SERIES

'A gripping, dark psychological thriller that delves even deeper into guilt, trauma and obsession. *Meet Me in the Darkness*, with its shocking, explosive opening, is a tense, deftly crafted game of hunter-and-hunted that will keep readers guessing to the final page'

DANIELLE RAMSAY, AUTHOR OF *THE PERFECT HUSBAND*

'Martta Kaukonen once again proves she's a *tour de force* in the psych thriller genre with this tautly plotted, highly original, twisty read. Her seamless execution keeps the reader turning the pages well into the night'

A.A. CHAUDHURI, AUTHOR OF *SHE'S MINE*

'A brilliant game of cat-and-mouse between author and reader. The pieces of this psychological thriller fit together as ingeniously as those in a Chinese puzzle box'

*THE TIMES*

'A tense, unsettling, gripping serial killer narrative that takes some very unexpected turns... Such a clever book!'

HARRIET TYCE, AUTHOR OF *BLOOD ORANGE*

'Surprising, fresh and almost indecently fun'

TAMMY COHEN, AUTHOR OF *THE WEDDING PARTY*

'A fascinating study in guilt, shame, blame and the stories we tell ourselves... The ultimate revelation of what has been going on in all four lives is horribly convincing'

*LITERARY REVIEW*

'Breathlessly plotted, deviously constructed, and brought to vivid, twisted life by an antiheroine for the ages… An utterly beguiling debut. This isn't just a thriller you sink your teeth into — it's a thriller that sinks its teeth right back into you'
ELIZABETH LITTLE, AUTHOR OF *DEAR DAUGHTER*

'Original, intelligent and intriguing — I gulped it down in two sittings'
ANDREA MARA, AUTHOR OF *NO ONE SAW A THING*

'An exciting, pacy page turner'        ALI KNIGHT, AUTHOR OF *BEFORE I FIND YOU*

'A gripping debut psychological thriller'        *GLAMOUR*

'This dark tale packs a punch when the deadly cat-and-mouse game culminates in a host of shattering revelations'        *IRISH INDEPENDENT*

MARTTA KAUKONEN lives in Helsinki. Before she became a full-time author, she was a film critic for Finland's biggest newspaper. *Follow the Butterfly* was her debut thriller—it was a critical and commercial hit in Finland, has been translated into fifteen languages, made the *Spiegel* bestseller list in Germany and is being adapted for a TV series. *Meet Me in the Darkness* is its sequel.

DAVID HACKSTON is a British translator of Finnish and Swedish literature and drama. He lives in Helsinki, where he works as a freelance translator. Notable publications include *Land of Snow and Ashes* by Petra Rautiainen, *My Cat Yugoslavia* by Pajtim Statovci and Martta Kaukonen's *Follow the Butterfly*, all available from Pushkin Press.

# MEET ME IN THE DARKNESS

## Martta Kaukonen

Translated from the Finnish by David Hackston

# ALSO BY THIS AUTHOR

## *Follow the Butterfly*


Pushkin Press
Somerset House, Strand
London WC2R 1LA





This work has been published with the financial support
of FILI – Finnish Literature Exchange.

A CIP catalogue record for this title is available from the British Library

The authorised representative in the EEA is eucomply OÜ,
Pärnu mnt. 139b-14, 11317, Tallinn, Estonia,
hello@eucompliancepartner.com, +33757690241

Designed and typeset by Tetragon, London
Printed and bound in the United Kingdom by Clays Ltd, Elcograf S.p.A.

This book is made of FSC-certified and recycled paper. The FSC-certified
materials meet FSC's standards for responsible forestry, and recycled
materials are used instead of virgin forest materials. www.fsc.org

www.pushkinpress.com

1 3 5 7 9 8 6 4 2

# MEET ME
## IN THE
## DARKNESS

HELSINKI 2023

# Ida

The axe's blade sank into my victim's forehead as though it had finally found its place in the world. The wooden handle jutted out like an extra limb.

How I loved the sight!

And how skilfully I'd made it happen! The axe had arched through the air like a falling star. A single blow, and the victim was dead.

Clean, considered, precise.

My murders were works of art! And I was their conscious *auteur*. I never settled for compromises.

If only you could have witnessed the magnificence of it all! But you can't, so you'll have to settle for my description.

Over the years, I've sent an impressive number of suits to an early grave. The list is so long that if people knew how many victims I'd actually claimed, they wouldn't believe it. How could I have killed so many people without getting caught?

These men toppled into their graves like dominos, as though their sole purpose in life was to be murdered by me.

Maybe it was.

Why are murderers never rewarded for their achievements?

I imagined myself on a podium—in first place, of course— taking a bow in front of a cheering crowd. Once the fanfares died down, I gave a speech. I thanked myself. I accepted the applause.

I snapped back to reality, to the victim's bedroom. I'd grabbed the designer lamp on the bedside table and was gripping it in my hand like a microphone.

I put the lamp back on the table, then raised my hands in front of my eyes and peered between my fingers. If you cropped the axe out of the picture, everything looked peaceful. My victim was lying in bed, relaxed. It was almost as though I'd put him out of a long, drawn-out misery.

If only he knew how dignified his death had been. I'll probably die of old age, ancient and worn-out. Unless I hire an assassin to take me out before I get there.

If I could just take a selfie alongside my creation… I wanted to immortalize the body and the axe. But I didn't want to fill my phone with incriminating evidence.

I felt the urge to press my bloodied fingers into my victim's cooling forehead, to leave my fingerprints as proof that it was me who had committed this murder, to make sure nobody else could take the credit for it or steal it from me.

But I didn't have time to hang around. I took a packet of disposable wipes from my bag, wiped down the foot of the lamp and the bedroom door handle. I hadn't touched anything else, and even then, I'd been wearing a pair of nitrile gloves. But you can never be too careful. By sticking to this principle, I'd never been caught for my crimes, and I wasn't planning on getting caught now either.

I glanced out of the window. A drunken man staggered out of the door of the Watering Hole across the street. I could have easily picked up another victim from the pub if I'd wanted to.

I hurried into the hallway.

Only then did I see it.

There among the dirty boots and old, misshapen trainers was a pair of pink suede high heels.

I only ever killed single men—and for good reason. I didn't want anyone to surprise me halfway through the butchering.

Was my victim married or just living with a girlfriend? Wife, lady friend—it didn't matter. The burning question was: where was his sweetheart now?

My jubilation was gone in an instant.

What if she'd heard us coming into the victim's apartment together? Or seen me take out the axe, got frightened and hidden somewhere?

Sweat tingled on my brow.

I'd never killed a woman.

And I didn't want to start now.

But there might be no avoiding it.

Was she hiding in the hallway? What if she was armed? A gun? Something heavy? An antique brass candlestick? A ten-kilo kettlebell that she could use to smash my kneecaps to a pulp?

I had to find her. I couldn't leave until I'd done so. What if she wasn't at home after all? In that case, I needed to get out of here before she came back.

Again, I took the axe out of my bag. I hadn't wanted to leave the murder weapon at the scene for the police to pore over. No, though it suited my victim's head perfectly.

I looked around. My eyes lighted on an old walnut wardrobe, the kind that led to Narnia.

I wrenched the door open. It was flimsier than I'd imagined, and I stumbled back at the lack of resistance. I gripped the door frame at the last minute and managed to stay upright.

I pushed the raincoats and gabardines to one side.

There was nobody in the wardrobe.

I moved on to the living room.

The space was dominated by a large, luxurious Chippendale sofa upholstered in black velvet. It was so low to the floor that there wasn't enough room underneath it for anybody to hide there. The peach-coloured curtains on either side of the windows were translucent. The bookcase was flush against the wall; no one could have squeezed in behind it. The room was empty.

Next was the kitchen.

The edge of the rose-decorated waxed tablecloth was short, so I didn't have to peer under the table. There was only one possible hiding place in the room, but even in the cleaning cupboard there was just a vacuum cleaner, a mop and a bucket.

The only place left was the bedroom. I clenched the axe in my sweaty hands and crept over the threshold.

The lady friend couldn't have been there either. Could she have witnessed her beau's demise without a peep? My victim had bellowed in horror as he'd seen the axe above his head.

But I had to inspect the room all the same.

I cautiously gripped the bedspread.

There was nobody under the bed.

The danger was over. Still, the victim's partner could turn up at any moment. I took out the wipes again and began hurriedly backing out of the apartment, quickly wiping all the surfaces I'd touched on my way.

I ran out of the apartment, down the staircase and all the way to the front door. I carried on running until I reached the bus stop. I needed to get out of Vallila, fast. I took the first bus that appeared, walked right to the back seat and sat down. It was only then that I realized my hands were trembling.

I'd never been that close to getting caught.

I glanced around. The bus was almost empty. Apart from me, there was nobody else sitting at the back.

From my bag, I took out a thick notebook and a ballpoint pen, and I started writing.

*The axe's blade sank into my victim's forehead as though it had finally found its place in the world.*

# Arto

I'd been preparing for my task carefully like a professional criminal. I was dressed in black, so that Ida wouldn't see me in the dark, and I was wearing a pair of woollen socks so I could move silently, like a rabbit. I'd got these socks for Christmas from my aunt, who had knitted them for me while she was in a home, but I'd bought the other clothes specifically for this purpose.

I tried to creep along the dark hallway as quietly as possible, all the way to the door to Ida's room.

The realization of what I was doing made me shudder.

Yet again, I had to convince myself, as I'd done many times before, that what I was doing was justified, that I didn't have any other options. After all, I was only trying to protect Ida, though in doing so I had to invade her privacy.

There was a mirror on the wall in the hallway. I automatically avoided it. I didn't want to see my run-down old figure, let alone the feeling that had made me this run-down in the first place written across my face. A feeling I'd tried to keep at bay, but which kept washing over me again and again, like waves in a storm.

Guilt, guilt, guilt.

Apart from the mirror, the only thing decorating the wall was our wedding photo in a simple wooden frame. Why hadn't I taken it down?

If Marja hadn't died prematurely, our marriage would inevitably have ended in divorce. But I'd never touched the photo, because I thought Ida might have happy memories of her mother and that she might want Marja to remain present in her life, even if only in a photograph.

My gaze fell on a faded paint stain on the floor.

Marja had died of cancer when Ida was just a child, but just before her death, she almost experienced a miraculous recovery—or at least that's what the doctor had predicted. Initially, the radiation therapy had seemed to work, and Marja was in such good condition that the doctor nearly sent her home from the hospital.

Upon hearing the news, I'd bought a tin of paint, and I was standing in the hallway, brush in hand, ready to paint the walls in Marja's favourite colour so she'd feel welcome when she returned to the battlefield of our marital disputes—and that's when my phone rang.

Marja's condition had deteriorated, and there was no longer any talk of sending her home, neither during that phone call nor later on. Instead, the doctor said if I wanted to see my wife again, I should get to the hospital as quickly as possible.

I dashed to the coat stand in the hallway and accidentally kicked over the tin of paint I'd just opened. The contents spilled over the threshold and into Ida's room. The stain always reminded me of Marja's death, but I'd never had the heart to get rid of it.

But besides Marja's death, the stain, which looked like a bunch of violets, reminded me that there was hope—unfounded hope, but hope all the same.

It turned out I needn't have hurried to the hospital after

all. Marja would struggle on for a long while yet, but I couldn't have known that.

I carefully gripped the door handle. It squeaked like a hungry cat. I hadn't oiled the hinges in years. My life was a series of things I should have taken care of but that I'd never got round to.

I lived amidst all that chaos. And I'm not talking about the chaos that had overtaken my mind, but the everyday jobs I should have taken care of but hadn't. Not since Marja had died.

I froze in front of the door. Had Ida heard the hinges creak? When the steady sound of the shower from the bathroom continued unbroken, I dared to slip into the room. I held my breath, as though Ida could have heard the air entering my lungs.

I stood in her room, and you can imagine I wasn't proud of myself. But, as I said, I only had her best interests at heart, even if it didn't quite seem that way.

Ida lived like a vampire. She had a habit of keeping the curtains closed even during the day. Outside the sun was shining, but the thick blackout curtains stopped so much as a single ray of light from getting through. I wanted to open the curtains to let at least a bit of sunshine into the room, but of course, I couldn't; that would have betrayed that I'd been there in the first place.

The room was as bare as a prison cell. A desk, a chair and a bookshelf: the same battered old pieces of furniture that Ida had kept in the cramped studio apartment where she'd lived before moving back in with me. Her bedside table was nothing but a tattered cardboard box, its lid covered in the rings left from countless mugs of tea. There wasn't even a bed, just a mattress on the floor. No posters, photographs or decorations that might reveal something about the character of the person who lived there.

But there was one exception.

On the wall above the mattress was a print.

*Live Love Laugh*

I hadn't asked Ida why she'd picked that particular print. But I knew my daughter well enough to realize it was an ironic joke on her part.

*Live Love Laugh*

Not exactly Ida's watchwords.

I quickly set about my task.

Razor blades. Scissors. Knives.

Every morning, after Ida had woken up and gone to the shower, I checked her room. I'd timed her showers and knew they lasted an average of six to seven minutes. I had an egg timer, with the volume turned down very low, set to go off in five minutes. As the minutes ticked away, I examined the room. I ran my hand under the thin futon mattress and felt around in case there was anything hidden underneath. I rummaged through the desk drawers that she and I had painted turquoise when she was a child. I stood on the wooden chair and reached up to check the top of the bookcase.

Nothing.

No razor blades. No scissors. No knives.

But I still didn't believe she had stopped cutting herself.

Or stopped contemplating suicide.

She and I had decided to move back in together four years ago. Her former therapist Clarissa Virtanen and her husband Pekka—or, as Ida called him, the Bastard—had recently been sentenced and imprisoned. With Clarissa as an accessory, the Bastard had first kidnapped Ida when she was only ten years old, and he did it again ten years later.

After all that had happened, Ida and I realized that now we needed to take care of each other. I'd started going to AA meetings and stopped drinking, while Ida was trying to come to terms with her trauma. Our living arrangements raised some eyebrows—a twenty-four-year-old, still living with her father—but I didn't care.

The egg timer buzzed. I could hear Ida stepping out of the bathroom and heading to the toilet. I crept up to the toilet door and listened. Had she gone in there to make herself sick? She had started slowly recovering from her eating disorder, but I still didn't believe she had put it behind her for good.

I stood there with my ear tight against the bathroom door, and a shadow of dreadful guilt once again darkened my mind. Why couldn't I trust my own daughter? She was trying her best to get better. I felt a pang in my chest at the thought that I wasn't the only one with trust issues.

Ida didn't trust me any more than I did her.

She was probably unaware of it, but I'd noticed she was in the habit of checking *my* room when I wasn't there. The mattress. The desk. The bookcase. She examined all the same places that I did when I went through her room. It wasn't hard to imagine that Ida knew I visited her room in precisely the same way.

Instead of razor blades, scissors and knives, she was looking for bottles.

She flushed the toilet, and I hurried back into the kitchen.

Ida glanced suspiciously at the porridge I'd made for her. Then she picked tiny spoonfuls from the edge of the bowl, avoiding the knob of butter, just as I'd expected.

We ate breakfast in silence. Our employer, *Helsinki Today*, took care of the conversation on our behalf. The paper rustled as I turned the pages. The following week, we were both to start working there: I as a summer reporter and she as an intern. I must have been the only summer reporter in the paper's history with a decades-long career to my name.

Again, I wondered how it was possible to be so close to someone yet still unable to make any contact with them. It was as though we were two astronauts drifting in outer space, both unaware of the other's existence. I wanted to put my arm around Ida's shoulder and tell her how much she meant to me, but our relationship wasn't like that, not any more, not since the Bastard had ruined everything.

Would I have been able to settle for those moments that I spent alone with her, or even feel happiness, if I'd known what we were about to experience together?

But I don't want to think of any of that yet.

Allow me to linger in the moment a while longer: Ida and I were sitting at the kitchen table in silence, and I missed her.

Neither of us had the faintest idea that fate had resolved to tear our lives to shreds one more time.

# Kerttu

Police Chief Tiilihella's expression was stern. Besides him, another five equally serious faces were staring at me. The portraits of Tiilihella's predecessors hung on the walls in fifty dreary shades of grey, their style glumly realistic, as if the artists had taken pains to emphasise that police work was nothing but joyless drudgery. The models in the paintings seemed to be competing to see who could look the dourest. But none of them could outdo the grimness of Tiilihella himself, sitting in front of me in the flesh.

Not even my father in his own portrait.

The only two things my father and I shared were our last name and our profession. My parents had assumed without question that I, too, would become a police officer. In my youth, I had taken up an apprenticeship as a hairdresser just to annoy them. I nearly lopped off a client's ear before admitting to myself that I had no choice but to follow in my father's footsteps.

Tiilihella's expression left nothing to the imagination. I almost expected him to say, 'Either agree, or I'll make you agree'. But there was no need. For Tiilihella, no meant no, and I had to accept that. I knew there was no point negotiating with him.

But I still tried.

Or perhaps I should say, begged. That's what my outburst sounded like, even to my own ears.

Tiilihella rammed his decision home by pounding his fist on the desk. A fist-shaped dent seemed to have appeared in the surface of the antique oak table that was Tiilihella's command post, doubtless from decades of similar blows. Clearly, I wasn't the only one who hadn't taken no for an answer right away. We police officers can be a stubborn bunch.

Tiilihella's eyes searched for something on his desk and eventually found it. He handed me a packet of cigarettes. He'd forgotten I was trying to give up. When I shook my head, he pulled one out, lit it and took a deep drag. I couldn't resist the temptation. I grabbed the pack, which he'd left on the desk, took a cigarette and asked him for a light.

I sought solace by looking out the window. Clouds drifted across the pale blue sky, free. I imagined climbing onto the roof of the Pasila police station and from there hopping onto a cloud. I would leave Pasila behind, and all my unsolved cases too. Tiilihella would see me from the window and shout after me, in vain. I'd wave to him, tear off a piece of the cloud and let it melt in my mouth like fluffy candyfloss.

Tiilihella had found me a quarter of an hour earlier in the dreary workplace canteen, where that day's lunch special was sausage soup. I had been sitting in my usual lonely spot—as I often did—eating and doing the crossword.

I'd just solved a clue: Nobel-winner, Pasternak, five letters. Literature wasn't my strongest suit, but I'd come across this one before: Boris. They say doing crosswords prevents memory loss, but I don't buy it. How could solving the same clues over and over help anyone at all?

Tiilihella had strode up to me, asked me to come to his office after lunch, and now here I was, suffering. I was struck once again by the thought that my boss had a brilliant psychological eye. The armchair I sat down in instantly humbled its occupant, as it was significantly lower than his own chair. I felt like a naughty girl in the headmaster's office. I had seen men much bigger than me sit in that chair with their knees up to their ears, while Tiilihella towered over them, his mouth set in a stern line. He certainly had his methods.

But I wouldn't back down.

Next to Tiilihella's desk was a bureau bearing a collection of framed photographs. In addition to his wife, the pictures showed his children and grandchildren. There were so many of them you might have thought Tiilihella belonged to some sect that forbade contraception. My bureau didn't have a single picture on it. I was grateful to all those who reproduced and populated the earth because, though the birth rate was plummeting, I had never fulfilled my civic duty.

Tiilihella began to write in his notebook, indicating that the matter was settled, and it was time for me to leave.

But I didn't budge.

I turned to admire the canvas hanging above the bureau, which I had painted as a gift for his fiftieth birthday. It depicted his summer cottage, where he and his wife Arja invited me to spend Midsummer every year. In it, Tiilihella was lying in a hammock, smiling blissfully, reading a thriller. It was the first painting I had ever given as a gift. I was still proud of it, though my technique had since improved enough that now I would have been able to make Tiilihella's eyes sparkle more brightly.

Tiilihella looked up from his notebook and seemed surprised to see me still sitting there. When he realized I had no intention of giving up, he sighed.

'Leppänen, my decision is final.'

His phone started to ring. It reminded me of an old trick people used to play on blind dates: ask a friend to call you half an hour in. If the date is a disaster, just lie and say you have to go, it's an emergency. Tiilihella picked up the phone with such a look of relief that I suspected this might have been his strategy too.

He was clearly pretending not to notice how furious I was about his decision.

I turned to a familiar mental exercise to quell my anger. I imagined lying on a white sandy beach in my safe place, listening to the waves of the turquoise sea lapping at the shore. This clichéd image from a holiday advertisement did its job, and I calmed down a little.

But only a little.

I shouted as I struggled to get out of the chair:

'You're making a mistake!'

If only I had known who would end up paying for that mistake.

Not Tiilihella.

But me.

# Ida

I heard my dad close the front door and rushed into his room.

I gripped the lid of my grandfather's old travelling chest, which bore the image of a mermaid, skilfully painted with a thin, delicate brush. The creature's seaweed-green tail looked like it was thrashing, as though someone had given her an electric shock. There used to be a wooden copy of the Little Mermaid standing in the garden outside Clarissa's surgery too.

I'd had the same dream countless times. In the dream, the mermaid and I dived down to the bottom of a muddy pond, but I never came back up to the surface.

Later on, I'd heard that the new owner of Clarissa and the Bastard's former house had chopped up the statue for firewood.

Whatever had happened to the outfit Clarissa had been wearing at the trial? It weirdly reminded me of Chanel's iconic suit, the one Jackie had been wearing the day JFK was shot. Only the pink pillbox hat and white gloves were missing. Her choice of attire wasn't a coincidence. Clarissa had wanted the reporters in the courtroom to think that her husband was an innocent victim and she was the long-suffering wife.

But when she thought nobody was looking, she winked at my dad like a coquettish Betty Boop.

That wink still wouldn't leave me in peace.

I'd sat on the couch in Clarissa's surgery numerous times, and I'd even believed she really wanted to help me. Instead, she and the Bastard had been plotting to kidnap me again.

I still couldn't believe it.

The lid of the chest was heavy as sin.

Or rather, heavy as all the sins I feared the chest might contain.

When I was a child, my dad used to hide all his secrets in here.

I lifted the lid with both hands. It banged against the wall.

I threw the worn-out socks and threadbare underpants on the floor. My dad had put them in there years ago. He assumed that, if I ever managed to open the chest, I'd lose interest once I saw them. But he was wrong. I'd first rummaged through the contents before I even went to school. But I'd always come away disappointed. I hadn't found jewels or golden coins. Back then, I hadn't realized that the treasures hidden within were far more valuable than that.

I took a porcelain cat out of the chest. My grandfather had brought it for my grandmother as a gift from one of his sea trips to Germany. The cat's surface was scratched from my playing with it. The figurine almost slipped from my sweaty hands, but I managed to hold it tight at the last minute.

Underneath the cat was a bundle of letters, tied together with a length of pink velvet ribbon. I'd been reading these letters since I was a teenager. At the time, I was shocked when I realized my parents had loved each other once.

I don't think even my dad remembered the warm feelings they used to have for each other. Or that he even wanted to remember them. I'd never heard him say a good word about my mother.

Maybe all that had existed between them was lust, not love at all. But how would I know? I've always had a hard time telling the two apart.

Suddenly I was gripping the handle of the axe again.

Its blade was red with blood.

Someone laughed.

It took a moment to realize that it was me.

Nobody was safe from me.

Not even my dad.

In the past, I used to be worried about doing things I hadn't actually done.

Now I was afraid I wouldn't be able to stop.

As if of its own accord, my hand reached up to my collar and slipped under my shirt. I caressed the key hanging around my neck on a thin silver chain.

I shook myself like a wet dog trying to dry its coat. That way, I was able to cling on to the here and now.

The room fell silent, and the axe disappeared from my hand.

I took an old photo album from the chest. I knew all the photos by heart. My dad as a young man. The girlfriends in his arms changed from picture to picture, and I could almost hear the sound of the old typewriter clacking away in his student digs.

A photograph slipped from between the pages and fell to the floor. I picked it up and slid it back into the album: my mum and dad pushing a pram through the park.

I wanted to find something that might tell me that my dad knew.

That he'd found out long before I did.

At the same time, I swore to God, to fate, to anyone. I swore I'd do anything for him not to know.

Underneath the photo album was a small parcel wrapped in tissue paper. The parcel contained a green silk dress. Next to this was a pair of electric-blue leather boots, their heels so tall that you could have seen into the neighbouring town while wearing them.

I was grateful to my dad for keeping this memory of my mum: the outfit she'd liked, maybe one that she'd worn to their first date or on the day they got engaged.

I wrapped the dress back in its silk paper.

Next up was a pile of blue-covered schoolbooks. The jotters fell from my hands and spread across the floor like a fan.

My dad had kept all his old school assignments. His stories were copies of the ones he'd read in the boys' books of his childhood: wild adventures on land, at sea and in the air. Maybe even as a schoolboy he'd dreamt of becoming a writer. But my mum had got there first. And once she'd published her first novel, my dad felt blocked. He couldn't write more than a sentence or two, let alone an entire book.

The chest was empty now. Nothing new had appeared there.

Relief washed over me like a tidal wave, but the sensation didn't last long.

I gave myself permission to take a deep breath, but my body refused to obey. Instead my breathing was shallow and shaky.

I started to place things back in the chest.

I felt the familiar rush. Enraged wasps bumping into one another inside me, waiting impatiently until they could sting me. I'd tried to tame them, but it was futile. They always ignored my commands.

If they wanted to attack someone, there was nothing I could do about it.

Four years is a long time.

In four years, our worst fears can come true.

In four years, a mouse can become a cat.

I no longer recognized my twenty-year-old self. How could such a timid creature have got the Bastard banged up for good?

But now, that wouldn't have been enough for me.

Now, I wouldn't have let him live.

# Arto

The chains on the swings creaked as two little girls started swinging faster, their laughter shrill and bright. Sheets hanging out to dry flapped in the breeze.

The sun gently tickled my face. If only I'd put on a T-shirt instead of a thick terry top.

I stood in the dimly lit park opposite an apartment block in Töölö and stared up at the window of the top-floor apartment as discreetly as I could.

A woman stepped out of the stairwell carrying a plastic bag full of empty bottles. I took a few steps to the side and into the shadow of an old spruce tree. It had started to shed some of its needles, but its thick branches were still full enough that they protected me from the glare of the sun. I glanced at my watch and tutted, feigning annoyance, as though I were waiting for someone who was very late.

I stepped out of the shadows to convince the woman I had nothing to hide, that I wasn't loitering in the park and had a perfectly good reason be standing there passing time. I think my little performance worked, as she took a phone out of her pocket and started scrolling through it with her free hand.

I turned and looked up at the window.

Ida had lived in that apartment before moving into my place. I used to stand in the park and watch my daughter's life through the windowpane. I couldn't bear seeing her slowly kill herself, so I'd settled for observing her from a distance instead.

Though Ida had moved out of this apartment years ago, I still found myself standing in the park from time to time. Perhaps it was force of habit that drew me there.

Every time I stood outside that building I was filled with the same fear and anxiety that I'd felt before. Every time I went there, I was afraid that she wouldn't appear at the window. To me, this could only have meant one thing: that she was dead.

It didn't matter that she might only have gone to the store or popped to the corner shop for some cigarettes.

Instead of ringing her doorbell, I would sit on the park bench for hours. Back then, I didn't have the strength to confront reality.

Now, that old fear was raising its head again. What if Ida's eating disorder were to spiral out of control again? What if I'd been too optimistic?

What magnetic force kept pulling me back to this same place?

The clouds had slowly glided in front of the sun, and it suddenly felt cold. Someone had left a redcurrant-coloured blanket on the bench; perhaps some kids had been playing with it. I felt like wrapping it around my shoulders, but if its owner came looking for it, I didn't want to have to explain why I was sitting shivering on a park bench wrapped in their blanket.

When I glanced at the blanket again, I noticed something glinting on the ground. It looked like a ring. I crouched down to look at it, but it was just some rubbish: the seal from a tin of sweets.

But next to the rubbish there was a four-leafed clover. I needed all the luck I could get! I picked it up and decided to press it in a pile of heavy books when I got home. I carefully slipped it into my wallet.

Again, I raised my eyes to the window.

The apartment was still empty. Ida hadn't allowed me to sell or rent it. For her, this apartment was like a back door. If living together didn't work out, she could always return to her miserable box room. And even though we'd managed to live under the same roof for four years now, she still wasn't ready to give up the apartment—I'd brought the matter up again only last week. That's how little she trusted me.

I sat down on the bench, took a copy of today's paper from my backpack and pretended to read it, in case the children thought I'd come to the park with darker intentions.

The girls left the swings and started running towards the building. I recalled what Ida used to look like when she was their age. To me, there was no sound sweeter than Ida's laughter when she was watching cartoons on television or when she and her best friend were playing with toy cars.

My phone rang. An unknown number. It was someone trying to sell me a new phone, so I ended the call quickly. In the past, I used to be worried any time someone called from an unknown number. I was convinced it must be the police calling to tell me that Ida had been found in her apartment, dead. That her eating disorder had finally gotten the better of her. Or worse still, that she had taken her own life.

I decided to head home. I folded the paper and put it in my backpack, then walked towards the park gate.

I stopped to open the gate but decided to look up at Ida's window one last time, as if to make sure she wasn't being held captive in her old apartment.

I turned and walked back to the bench.

I looked up at the window.

A figure appeared from behind the curtains.

I froze on the spot.

I stood there like a pillar of salt. The minutes passed.

Only then did I conclude that I must have been mistaken. There couldn't be anybody in the apartment.

Not even Ida's ghost, though I could have sworn my daughter had gazed out of that window and looked me right in the eyes only a moment ago.

# Kerttu

Tiilihella had just rejected my application for retirement, though we had agreed this in writing over a year ago. A case had just arrived on the police desk, a case so challenging that he believed nobody else could get to the bottom of it but me, Kerttu Leppänen, detective superintendent of the murder unit and director of the Violent Crimes Unit of the Helsinki constabulary.

I already had one foot in the doorway. It was no wonder my mind was teeming with memories of my lengthy career. I was constantly mulling over old cases. I even lay awake at night ruminating about things, unless I was able to fall asleep, and even then I dreamt of the past.

A regular guest in my dreams was Janne Metsäkankare, the victim in my first homicide investigation, a man whose autopsy I had attended at the beginning of my career decades ago and whose screams I still heard in my nightmares.

I'd never got over the case, primarily because it remained unsolved. And it would stay unsolved when I retired, and soon nobody would remember Janne. All my other colleagues who had worked on the case had retired long ago. Even Timo Päre, the coroner who had conducted the autopsy, had been dead for years.

I can imagine your reaction. An unsolved murder. How awful! And it is awful, but—Janne's murder wasn't the only unsolved murder weighing down my conscience. You'll be familiar with some of them from the media. Every police officer has unsolved cases to their name—'cold cases', as we call them. It's inevitable.

The Finnish police force has over two hundred unsolved homicides from the last fifty years. Of course, not all of them were my cases. And some of them—including Janne's murder—have been forgotten over the years, overshadowed by more salacious media-fodder.

Janne's parents had died in a car crash caused by a drunk driver soon after their son's death. I was the only person left who cared about his fate. That's what it felt like, though I knew it wasn't true.

One more month and then I would be free. I would finally be able to do all the things I kept moving into the 'Once I'm retired' folder: take a woodwork course at the adult education centre, go hiking in Lapland during the autumn, buy a motorbike and ride around aimlessly for as long as I liked.

I closed my eyes and envisaged the workbench, the fells ablaze in autumnal colour, the asphalt stretching out as far as the eye could see.

But no.

At first, I didn't even notice that my eyes were again drawn to the grey linoleum flooring that nobody had thought fashionable since the 1980s. The linoleum had curled in the right-hand corner of the room. It too was trying to escape my office, with about as much success as me. I felt an affinity with that flooring. I vowed that if I ever managed to get out of here and put the Pasila police station behind me, I would never set foot in here again and I'd avoid the whole neighbourhood like the plague.

All the items of furniture in my office were original, from 1982, the year the station was built. The roller-door cabinet that nobody else knew how to open but me. The dented filing cabinet that I used to take out my frustration on by kicking the lowest drawer. The sleek bureau that looked a little out of place among all the battered old office furniture. The fluorescent strip on the ceiling, chirping like a grasshopper, and the flies it had grilled long ago that sometimes fell on my neck.

My phone rang. Tiilihella had forgotten something.

The media must not find out about the case that had scuppered my retirement plans.

I'd already thought perhaps I ought to enlist the help of my trusted hack Arto Haaleajärvi. Of course, I had all kinds of contacts in the criminal underworld, but Arto's network was on an altogether different level. Throughout his career, he'd written about many subjects besides crimes, but I knew that criminals always turned to him first when they felt like talking. Arto had handed me a whole host of lawbreakers in return for some juicy scoops.

A journalist should never reveal his sources, but neither should police officers leak details of ongoing investigations to journalists. I'd always managed to hide Arto's involvement so that the criminals had no idea what was about to hit them.

Arto may well have heard a thing or two about the case. Right now, I needed every speck of information, no matter how small.

But Tiilihella's word was the law.

I took a small mirror out of my handbag and looked at my reflection. This is what a disappointed, frustrated person looks like. I wondered how best to represent these emotions in a painting. I would highlight the sagging corners of my mouth, the resignation in my eyes. The numerous wrinkles around my eyes and mouth would require a finer brush. I looked considerably older than my years, especially as I hadn't bothered to dye my greying hair or put on any make-up.

There was a knock at the door. My subordinate Sergeant Nikulainen opened the door and peered inside before stepping into the room. His cheeks were glowing red, and his gaze was fixed on the floor. His constant shyness really got on my nerves.

It was as if he was afraid of me.

'Come in! I won't bite.'

'I got the photos developed.'

He handed me an envelope, then slipped out of the room as though he had never been there and closed the door behind him.

The crime-scene photos.

I hadn't even opened the envelope when there was another knock at the door.

I recognized this knocker from the knock. Chief Inspector Koivuvyö had already heard what had happened and had come to jeer at my misfortune. I almost felt like pretending I wasn't there.

I ordered Koivuvyö into the office very loudly, making my irritation clear to all my colleagues with an office along the same corridor.

Koivuvyö stepped inside.

'Kert—'

I interrupted him.

'To you, I am Leppänen. In your free time, you can call me whatever you like, but when you're on duty I am your boss, and you will address me as Leppänen.'

Koivuvyö gave a smirk.

'Are you deaf or just plain stupid?' I boomed. 'We agreed this on your very first day here.'

Koivuvyö had started working under my supervision five years ago. He was slightly younger than me and had an impressive career in Turku to his name. He had been promised a promotion, but he'd had enough of his long-distance relationship and wanted to move to Helsinki, where his partner lived, before he retired.

His smirk still hadn't disappeared. My anger didn't faze him. He and I had argued countless times, and it shames me to admit, but I had behaved even worse towards him than this. He was in urgent need of some discipline, but he didn't see me as an authority figure.

'What's this about?'

I asked this question so loudly that my words echoed around the office. Koivuvyö pretended not to notice.

Before losing my temper even further, I performed another mental exercise. I picked up a handful of sand baked in the sun and slowly let it run between my fingers.

My breath began to steady again.

Once I retired, perhaps I would be able to travel to the landscape of my meditation exercises, to a desert island where the waves lap gently against the shore and the sand is almost as soft as snow. In my mind, I'd been returning to that landscape for over a year now.

If I was ever able to retire, that is.

'This just came back from the lab.'

Koivuvyö was holding a parcel as though he owned it. He didn't want to give it up; he wanted to examine it himself.

'Is this the one?'

I was surprised to hear that a note of enthusiasm had crept into my voice.

Koivuvyö handed over the parcel and looked at it longingly.

'Off you go!'

Koivuvyö gave another smirk as he walked to the door, almost in slow motion. Once in the doorway, he cast me a final mischievous glance. He disappeared, leaving the door ajar. I kicked it shut.

I could feel the familiar tingling on my skin.

I wanted to solve this case once and for all.

But right then, I didn't know what I was going to lose in the process.

# Ida

I sat at home, alone, reading my old diaries. Hundreds of pages of pain and anxiety. My dad had gone to meet an old friend, and a sense of loneliness had consumed me.

I decided to go for a pint at the Quill and Parchment, a pub popular with the staff at *Helsinki Today*.

It was still light outside though it was almost ten o'clock. In front of the railway station, three fast-food vans stood in a row, giving off the nauseating smell of fried sausage and cooking fat. I decided to have a shower as soon as I got home, as I could almost feel the grease seeping into my skin and hair.

The pub was full of thirsty journos, as it always was on a Friday evening. My dad's colleagues, who had known me since I was a kid.

There was a queue at the bar. I heard someone say my name. I glanced around, but nobody seemed to have come up to talk to me. A moment later, I heard my name again. I noticed two familiar figures propping up the bar with their backs to me: the editors-in-chief of rival tabloids. Neither of them had noticed me.

They were just talking about me.

For once, there was something these two rivals could agree on. Apparently, appointing me as an intern at *Helsinki Today* was unethical. I was a victim of a serious crime, and *Helsinki Today*'s editor Ari Visalahti was only using me.

These editors thought my appointment was nothing but a PR stunt: the daughter of the famous novelist Marja Simpukka, victim in a notorious abuse case, joins top newspaper. But they didn't seem to think it would attract many new readers.

The fact that I'd agreed to it proved that I didn't know what was in my own best interests. I was easily manipulated. Why hadn't my dad intervened?

One of the editors suggested I probably needed some kind of legal guardianship.

And he was probably right.

I finally got my pint. The editors continued moralizing. I was certain that if they had been the ones to come up with the idea of offering me an internship, they wouldn't have found my appointment at all questionable. This was just sour grapes.

Luckily, the table in the furthest corner of the bar was free. I threw my leather jacket over the back of the chair, opened up the copy of *Helsinki Today* that had been left folded on the table and quickly skipped past the crime news.

I'd already reached the comics section when the clack of high heels almost drowned out Amy Winehouse's story of rehab, which was playing in the background.

Irmeli Lahjametsä was standing next to me.

Of course, I shouldn't have been surprised. The Quill and Parchment was Irmeli's local haunt too, but I hadn't seen her since Clarissa and the Bastard's trial four years ago. I suppose I'd assumed I would never see her again.

Irmeli had retired a few weeks before the trial. She was still in court to follow the proceedings, but mostly to take care of me and my dad. Her violet wig was the first thing I saw every day when I arrived at the courthouse. She had the habit of waiting for me and my dad in the foyer, then she steered us past the crowds of ravenous hacks and photographers and into the courtroom, as though she were a steroid-fuelled bodyguard and not a cancer-riddled waif. I only realized much later that I would never have survived the trial without her motherly care and protection.

Irmeli used to be my mother's best friend. And she wasn't just looking after me out of a sense of duty to her dead friend; I was like her very own child. She had no children of her own—'but not by choice,' she always added.

My dad hadn't wanted Irmeli to follow the trial. He'd said she had a purely professional interest in the case, but this wasn't true, because she never wrote a word about the trial.

It wasn't hard to guess the real reason my dad had objected to her presence there: he didn't want her to hear all the details of the case. He blamed himself for what had happened to me, and he was afraid that everybody else would blame him too.

Irmeli still had a surprising amount of influence. I knew that she had convinced Visalahti to hire me and my dad at *Helsinki Today*. In the end, Visalahti had called my dad out of the blue and invited us for an interview.

She pulled me towards her and gave me a hug. Her shoulder blades protruded like an angel's wings. I was worried her illness might have recurred. I wanted to ask whether she was clear, but I couldn't. I couldn't have coped if she'd told me the doctor had given her a death sentence.

Tears welled in my eyes.

'It's been a while.'

Irmeli lowered her eyes. Was she ashamed of not keeping in touch with me? I started to feel ashamed too.

I'd missed her terribly, but I'd thought it was her job to contact me because she was the one who had pulled off the perfect disappearing act. But my stubbornness felt stupid now. We hadn't seen each other for years, just because I'd been so childish and proud.

'It really has! I saw you in passing the Sunday before last, I was driving and tried to wave. You probably didn't notice me.'

Anxiety clenched my chest. I'd been trying not to think about that evening. Why did she have to dig up something I'd hoped had started to decompose long ago?

'I haven't been anywhere for ages. My dad and I have mostly been spending the evenings at home.'

The Sunday before last had been fourteen years to the day since the Bastard had first snatched me. I wasn't able to think about anything else.

No, I really wasn't myself that evening. And that's exactly why I'd done something I would never otherwise have done.

Or would I?

What if I was just looking for excuses so I could live with myself?

How much did Irmeli really know?

'I could have sworn it was you! It must have been around nine thirty in the evening. You were leaving the Watering Hole with a man.'

Irmeli was used to teasing the truth out of her interviewees, sometimes by force. Nobody was afforded any mercy, neither corrupt politicians nor amoral CEOs. It was no wonder that she'd won the Finnish Journalism Award twice in two different categories. But she would not break me.

'I'd be able to pick you out of a police line-up!' Her laugh sounded fake.

My laughter sounded fake too. It caught in my throat.

'You can ask my dad, if you don't believe me.'

I was confident that she never would.

And why would she? She wasn't a police officer.

And I wasn't a suspect.

My dad would surely give me an alibi, if necessary.

Irmeli's laugh was cut short. She looked serious. But she couldn't know anything? Could she?

'It was you, Ida.'

Why couldn't she just believe me? I'd never lied to her before. Irmeli was known for her tenacity; she never left a stone unturned. What if she started investigating the matter further?

If Clarissa and the Bastard were found to be *non compos mentis*, then so would I.

Irmeli had had enough. She looked daggers at me, mouthed a curt 'bye' and headed to the counter.

I hurried to get out of the bar. I didn't want her to come back to my table and start ranting on again.

She was waiting for her drink at the bar. I had to walk past her. I tried to slip by without her noticing, but she turned to me.

'You were wearing that same leather jacket.'

She had a memory like an elephant. She used to brag that she never had to record her interviews but just took notes. And to prove it, she would recite lengthy monologues word for word. But still. Could she really remember what I'd been wearing almost two weeks ago? She'd only seen me in passing through her car window.

I said nothing.

I would have to get rid of that jacket. Someone else could have seen me too. An eyewitness might be able to describe the jacket to the cops.

I took a long, slow breath, then exhaled. In, out, slowly, to steady my pulse, to calm the blood rushing through my veins like a churning sea.

I pressed a hand against my chest. The key warmed my palm.

I mustn't start thinking about blood.

Or the axe.

And certainly not the bloody axe.

But what about Irmeli?

What should I do about her?

# Arto

The sea of garish red flowers was heaving so much that I felt as though I'd been shipwrecked and was being buffeted around without a life vest. The enormous paintings covering the walls at Kiasma were like psychedelic murals. If you asked me, they would have been more suited to a high-school summer exhibition than the most eminent contemporary art museum in the country. People used to joke that a child would have been able to paint a more realistic rose than this artist.

The sight continued out into the museum's courtyard. Standing on the lawn were potting boxes filled with different-coloured roses. Luckily, they were only on display temporarily; I'd never really cared for roses. They reminded me of people's duplicity: even the most beautiful rose has thorns.

When it came to Rosa Purple, I couldn't understand what all the fuss was about. Since her death four years ago, it seemed the whole country felt duty-bound to worship her.

Anne Hiltunen, an art historian specializing in Rosa Purple's work, had written an article for *Helsinki Today*'s Sunday supplement about the significance of the great artist's work for Finnish art. Hiltunen went so far as to suggest that Purple was Finland's answer to Yayoi Kusama, a wild, unbridled gift to the Finnish art world. Apparently the two artists had much in common, such as their bold approach to colour and the humorous eye they cast on the world around them.

I'd suggested that Ida and I visit the exhibition and see these paintings together. She wasn't interested in red roses any more than I was. However, alongside the retrospective of Purple's work, Kiasma was also running an exhibition on the anarchistic work of Purple's son, the performance artist Roni Lahtinen. Even at the age of forty-seven, Lahtinen was still the *enfant terrible* of performance art, still an angry young man. His admirers were taken as much by his works as his rock-star appearance. The last time I'd heard about Lahtinen was when he'd given an interview in *Helsinki Today* shortly after his mother's death, saying he was putting together a performance around the theme of #MeToo.

The auditorium was showing short clips of Lahtinen's works, while the artist himself was to be found standing in the exhibition hall beside what was perhaps Purple's most famous painting: *Farewell to Roses*. Everyone in Finland recognized that painting. For years now, the familiar roses had been reprinted on napkins, curtains, you name it. There probably wasn't a household in the land that didn't have a set of sheets or tablecloths with these flowers on them.

Lahtinen was staring at the lower right-hand corner of the painting. Something was obviously amiss, but I didn't under-stand what. I tried to peer over his shoulder to see what could be so interesting that it had caught his attention like this, but I couldn't see anything out of the ordinary. To me, the roses looked exactly the same as the ones on the tablecloth that Marja had bought. I'd laughed when she spread it across our kitchen table—*could there be anything more middle class?* Every petal, every thorn and bud was in just the right place.

Lahtinen was wearing a pair of skinny black jeans and a studded leather jacket. He and Ida shared a penchant for that moody look. His T-shirt was a dirty grey, literally. I imagined it might once have been white, but it had probably never been washed. He fidgeted with the large safety pin he'd stuck through his earlobe and ruffled his black-dyed hair. He looked uneasy.

I turned around, theatrically rolling my eyes at his pretentiousness, but Ida had disappeared.

Eventually, I found her sitting in the back row of the auditorium. The room was almost full, and people sat watching the film in silence. The screen flickered with a hundred scarpering cats. Police desperately running after them with nets in their hands. My ears were ringing from the creatures' incessant caterwauling. A furious policeman swore in German as he cuffed Lahtinen. A grotesque tattoo of a skull could be seen under the sleeve of the artist's weather-worn leather jacket as the policeman grabbed him roughly and started dragging him towards the awaiting police van.

The suspect didn't resist arrest but got into the van voluntarily. For a moment, Lahtinen's hysterical laughter echoed around the shopping centre's forecourt until the officer finally slammed the van door shut.

This was Lahtinen's most controversial work, one that he had pulled off while living in Berlin. He had collected dozens of cats from different shelters across Germany, then released them all at once outside a Berlin shopping centre. The event led to a tightening of Germany's animal-protection laws, and Lahtinen was slapped with a fine for vandalism.

The video came to an end, and the audience began to file out of the auditorium. I stood by the stage and waited for Ida, and we returned to the room full of Purple's work. Lahtinen was still standing in front of his mother's painting; he hadn't moved. As we walked past him on our way to the front door, he turned and looked at us. It was obvious that he recognized Ida instantly.

Lahtinen stared at her as though he was admiring a work of art. Ida gave a cautious smile.

Lahtinen started to walk towards us, still staring at my daughter as though he intended to swallow her whole. I shuddered as though the hand of death had just pointed a finger at me.

'Did you like the exhibition?'

Lahtinen had been twiddling the safety pin in his ear so much that it had started bleeding.

'The thing with the cats was interesting. I…'

I put an arm around Ida and guided her towards the exit, half running. She tried to struggle free, but I wouldn't let her.

A father doesn't normally have to protect his twenty-four-year-old daughter. I'd failed at protecting Ida when she was a child. I'd decided I would never let anything bad happen to her again.

But I knew there were still monsters on her heels.

# Kerttu

The murdered boy's scream, laced with despair, rang in my ears. I heard it just as clearly as I had decades ago. I lay in bed and knew I wouldn't be able to fall asleep. My mind was racing with memories of my first murder case and its victim Janne Metsäkankare.

The boy's body had been lying in front of me on a metallic gurney, his chest open, the forensic pathologist Timo Päre holding his heart.

I had gripped my pen and notepad, where I was supposed to take notes about observations made during the course of the autopsy. After all, I was the main detective on the case.

If Päre had looked away, I would have hugged the boy, or at least gripped his hand and pressed it against my chest. Of course, I didn't know whether the deceased wanted to feel my heartbeat now that his own heart had stopped. Meanwhile, my heart was pounding like the little drummer boy beating his tin drum. *Tum tum tum!*

I had imagined myself and the boy in a pietà position: his languishing, emaciated body in my arms and my tears moistening his innocent face. But though suffering had left its mark on him, he hadn't exactly been Jesus Christ during his life, and I certainly wasn't the Virgin Mary!

I had wanted to assure him that everything would be all right. In a way, this was true. All the evil was behind us now, and his worst fears had already come true. I wasn't a priest; I didn't even believe in God, so I couldn't promise him a place in heaven. But what was certain, however, was that his suffering and whatever it was that he had experienced was over now. How could I have convinced him of that?

The boy's long hair framed his pale face. Again, this reminded me of Jesus. But this boy was not going to rise from the dead, neither on the third day nor afterwards.

His death had been inevitable: an unavoidable fact, a boulder impossible to walk around or to climb over.

Blood had dripped from the heart and onto the tiled floor of the autopsy room. With all the constant scouring, the tiles were now almost grey.

Later that evening, the cleaners would mop the floors and hose the boy's blood down the drain. Only a day earlier, that blood had been doing what it was supposed to, carrying oxygen and nutrients to different parts of his body. Now his blood was nothing but waste, red and white cells that no longer had any function. For some reason, this thought made me even sadder than the sight of his now redundant body.

The scream filled the room. The fluorescent lamps on the ceiling had started to flicker in my eyes, as if someone had been standing there switching them on and off, over and over again. The smell of sulphur was so pungent that I almost had to gasp for breath.

The scream faded just as suddenly as it had begun and turned to silence so quickly that a seed of doubt appeared in my mind, making me wonder whether I'd ever heard the scream in the first place.

The boy's body was still where it had been. I don't know what I'd been expecting. Perhaps to see him leap to his feet and shout, 'Surprise!', as though his death had been nothing but a cruel practical joke.

Päre was still holding the heart and explaining to me in an officious tone why the boy's death must have been a violent one. It seemed Päre had not heard anything, or maybe he was so accustomed to the screams of the dead that he no longer reacted to them at all.

Eventually, he managed to tell me everything I needed to know about the victim's heart, then he turned to look at me, as if to make sure I had understood what he had said. I nodded as firmly as I could. I was already worried that Päre planned to hold a viva about the condition of the heart and that I would fail this miserably, but he had put it back in its metallic bowl, placed a hand on the victim's liver and begun presenting his thoughts on how it had been damaged.

All of a sudden, I had come crashing back to reality. I felt weak. The episode—or whatever you'd like to call it—had drained all my strength.

My hospital sandals pushed against the tiled floor. The air conditioning pumped fresh air into the room, cooling my sweaty face. From the corridor came the even hum of a vacuum cleaner. I was here. Here and now.

I was finally able to focus on the pathologist's words. The liver damage revealed that someone had struck the victim in the gut with a blunt object or kicked him, probably hit him too. Splinters had been found on the victim's T-shirt that could have come from the two-by-four found next to his body. There had been blood on the wood, probably that of the victim, but that would have to be established in the lab. Päre imitated the blow by pretending to hit me with an imaginary length of wood. I instinctively flinched and moved out of the way.

But the victim had been kicked too, right in the face. This was revealed in his fractured jaw, his broken front tooth and an eye tooth that had come out altogether. Päre showed me the small plastic jar in which he had preserved the latter. He had assumed that the blow must have caused the victim to fall on his back, and that the killer had only kicked him in the face once he was lying on the ground, unconscious. Päre suspected that the cause of death must have been brain damage sustained from that very kick.

I had spent the night before that autopsy all those decades ago having visions of bloodied, severed limbs, crushed skulls, visions that I had no desire to remember and that are too unpleasant to describe here.

However, not even those shocking visions could have prepared me for what I had encountered only hours later in the autopsy room.

Of course, this wasn't the first time I had watched an autopsy—I had attended many during my student days—but this was the first murder case in which I was going to be the lead investigator.

Päre had said all he was going to say and had tried to take my hand as he said goodbye. He didn't succeed, because I was still clutching my pen and notepad where I hadn't written a single word.

It was only once I had left the autopsy room that I realized what had actually happened in there.

Janne had called out the name of his killer.

# Arto

The corners of editor-in-chief Ari Visalahti's mouth were so tight I was worried they might rip.

The editorial team at *Helsinki Today* had taken some time out of their busy schedule to welcome me and Ida on our first day at work. We were all standing around the round table in the conference room waiting for the editor-in-chief to sink the cake server into the Princess Cake, whose green marzipan coating gleamed like a stick of uranium.

The cake revolted me, but I decided to force myself to have just a small piece so that Visalahti wouldn't think I had a hangover.

Visalahti managed to scoop a slice of cake onto a small plate and offered it to Ida, still with that fake smile. Ida recoiled from it, as if the cake might have been absorbed into her body if she stood too close to it. Our colleagues looked down at their shoes in embarrassment.

I snatched the plate from Visalahti's hand. He hurriedly began serving more slices and handing plates to all those who wanted one.

The awkward situation reminded me that, no matter what I kept trying to tell myself, Ida hadn't yet fully recovered.

Why couldn't my daughter be normal?

What a terrible thing to think!

How could I be ashamed of my own daughter, especially

as I knew that the trauma she had experienced was what had caused her illness in the first place!

Again, I wondered what kind of father I'd been. I was a complete and utter failure as a parent.

I picked up the spoon and shoved the radioactive mass into my mouth.

Visalahti's spoon clinked against his coffee cup and the murmur of conversation died down. I was worried that he might be about to make a speech welcoming us to the editorial team, but he just raised his cup as if it were a champagne flute and wished us good luck. Our colleagues raised their cups too and mumbled their greetings.

I was unsure how Ida and I would survive in the office if the atmosphere was always this fraught.

Once we'd finished our cake, Visalahti invited us into his office.

The walls were lined with boxes.

'As you know, I've only recently started here. I haven't had a chance to unpack yet.'

He ushered us to sit at his desk while he remained standing by the window.

A seagull swooped in front of the window, as if it was deciding whether to off itself by flying into the tower of glass. I knew the feeling and felt great sympathy for the bird.

'Let's agree that you'll be Ida's mentor, show her the ropes.'

I'd already internalized Visalahti's jargon, so I knew that what he really meant was that I could rewrite Ida's stories, in case it turned out my daughter was illiterate.

Ida turned to me. She looked cheerful. She hadn't understood what the editor-in-chief really meant; she was just happy I'd be there to 'show her the ropes'. I felt sorry for her.

Visalahti led us out of his office.

'Ida, let me give you the guided tour.'

My daughter probably knew this building better than he did; she used to play with her toy cars under my desk when she was a toddler. Visalahti showed us the desk of every reporter and photographer in the open-plan office. It was only then that I noticed my former desk had been taken and that sitting in my chair was the new political correspondent. I assumed the new columnist would pack up and move right away, but Visalahti continued to walk us through the space.

He proudly presented us a pompous framed photograph displayed on the wall. Taken in the mid-1920s, the then editorial staff of *Helsinki Today* was immortalized sitting around a table at the Torni restaurant, laughing convivially. I was reminded of all the liquid lunches I'd enjoyed at my employer's expenses in my heyday.

'*Helsinki Today* has a long history. You should bear that in mind every time you write a piece.'

That was Visalahti's way of reminding me that I couldn't afford to screw up any more.

To round off our tour, he ushered us to the furthest corner of the office, where two desks had been set up for us, like disobedient school children sent to the corner to think about what they had done. Ida was relieved that we were sitting out of other people's sight.

'You'll be writing your first pieces today.'

I knew editorial were only going to throw us crumbs to start with. The kind of news stories the other reporters didn't want to waste their time with.

It was understandable that they wanted Ida to start with the basics—after all, she had no experience of being a reporter, and no work experience at all, for that matter—but for an old-timer like me, starting from scratch again was a knock to my self-esteem.

The last time I'd written stories about fights at the all-night diner and drunks playing tag with knives was when I was a rookie in my twenties. The kind of stories that you forget before you'd even finished writing them up. Deaths that interest nobody except the next of kin, and oftentimes they didn't care either.

There was a time when my reports, exposés and interviews with celebrities were the main reason people bought *Helsinki Today*. I wasn't allowed to mess up. I was expected to come up with the kinds of stories our competitors could only dream about.

Stress had always been a good excuse to hit the bottle. So were the scoops.

I decided that from now on Ida and I would write each and every one of our stories with as much care and attention as if we were writing up the scoop of a lifetime.

I'd betrayed her trust on countless occasions. Now I had a chance to help her.

At least, that's what I thought at the time. There was no way I could have known what kind of lion's den our work was about to lead us into.

# Ida

I was sitting in a crowded bus on my way to work. To pass the time, I was listening to a podcast about my case, and the rasping voice of Piia Korsisuo filled my ears. *Guilty As Charged* was by far the most popular true-crime podcast in Finland, and listeners knew that Korsisuo always stood up for the victims. I begged to differ. She hadn't contacted me in advance to warn me that she was planning an episode about my case. Then suddenly, out of the blue, my face was on posters at bus stops, in the metro station and on trams advertising the programme.

Of course, Korsisuo's podcast wasn't the first such piece about my case. And it surely wouldn't be the last.

Korsisuo had really gone into the details. She had all the facts. But it still made me sick that other people got to draw their own conclusions about my life and the worst things I'd ever experienced. Each time, I had to go through those experiences again and again. But that didn't seem to interest anybody.

Korsisuo reached the conclusion that Clarissa must have had me fooled. But maybe it was my own fault that she interpreted my relationship with Clarissa like that. I'd only told the court a fraction of what had really happened.

Besides, it was silly to blame Korsisuo. At least she thought she was on the victims' side. The same certainly couldn't be said for most people who had investigated my case.

Right now, she was interviewing a criminologist who, trying to muster all the authority of expertise, was attempting to explain how it was possible that the Bastard hadn't been caught sooner. I really wanted to know that too. But sadly, the criminologist's explanation wasn't all that convincing.

I couldn't concentrate any more. My attention was drawn to a group of teenage girls sitting in front of me. They were whispering to one another and peering over their shoulders. One of them had braces that made her hiss like wind in the reeds. It wasn't hard to guess what they were gossiping about. And before long, one of them pulled out her phone and snapped a picture of me, as if I wouldn't notice.

I decided to pretend nothing had happened.

Thankfully it was only one more stop until I got to work. I managed to get off the bus before anyone else decided to take pictures of me.

Andy Warhol was wrong when he said everybody would have fifteen minutes of fame. My fame had already lasted four years, and there was no end in sight. I didn't think I'd done anything interesting enough to deserve all the attention.

In fact, I hadn't done anything at all. The Bastard had done everything, aided and abetted by Clarissa. I was just an object.

This was the first time I'd had the courage to go to work without my dad. My first days were an amorphous blur; everything seemed to repeat from one day to the next.

My dad and I always arrived at the office at around nine o'clock. We had a cup of coffee at our respective desks, then waited for the police to send the media a press release about a death that would elicit a mere five lines of text in *Helsinki*

*Today*. For the most part, all we ever reported on were assaults and burglaries.

Every evening, I was relieved that nobody had died. But my dad could hardly conceal his boredom. He was used to being in the thick of things, the first on the scene of an accident or a police stand-off. Nothing had happened in my life for a long time. For the last few years, I'd mostly been at home, so sitting still and twiddling my thumbs wasn't exactly a problem for me. My dad, meanwhile, rocked back and forth on his chair and fidgeted with his phone.

I walked from the bus stop to the entrance of the glass skyscraper. To my surprise, I was the first person to arrive at the office. I switched on the lights, walked to my desk and booted up my computer.

My case had kept the crime reporters busier than any other for decades. And now the readers of *Helsinki Today* were able to read crime reports written by the most famous victim in Finland: 'Ida the Psycho Shrink Survivor', as the media had called me since the trial.

I wondered if I'd received any post. I started watching cat videos but couldn't even concentrate on them. My cuticles started bleeding. I'd been pulling at them again without even noticing. I looked at the time. The others would be arriving soon. I went to my post box. A parcel had arrived for me. I picked it up and walked back to my desk, then looked for a pair of scissors in the drawer and opened the parcel. Inside was something wrapped in pink foil, like a Valentine's gift. I lifted the foil out of the box and unwrapped it.

I screamed.

A heart.

I closed my eyes. Opened them again.

The heart hadn't disappeared. I could almost hear its beating, though of course it wasn't beating any more. Not since it had been dug out of its owner's chest.

I pushed the box away.

In primary school, there was a poster on the wall explaining human anatomy. The image on the poster was black-and-white, except for the heart which was bright red. The heart wrapped in foil reminded me of the anatomy poster so much that it was almost absurd.

I ran to the toilet and threw up.

I returned to my desk and googled the words *human heart*.

I found out that the human heart is smaller and doesn't weigh as much as the one sent to me.

I frantically wiped my eyes and cheeks and googled again. The heart in the box belonged to a cow.

What was the sender trying to tell me?

One thing was certain: the sender was a man.

Just like all the others who tried to get close to me.

Was this heart meant as a proposal? He certainly wouldn't have been the first man to become infatuated with me.

I didn't understand why you would want to date someone that you knew was completely broken. But these men weren't interested in me; they were interested in my *case*. These were true-crime freaks. What better way to get to see the investigation close-up than by dating the victim!

I hadn't wanted the trial to be held behind closed doors. I hadn't done anything wrong. I had nothing to be ashamed of. Nonetheless, the judge had decided that some of the documents would be kept confidential. He had no choice, as the trial touched upon some of Clarissa's other patients.

The suitors seemed to imagine I could help them get their hands on these classified documents; that we'd first have sex, then lie in bed and go through the transcripts from Clarissa's interviews.

I reached for my key, ran my fingers along its grooves.

Did the sender want to let me know I'd be next?

My heart was beating what felt like its last beats.

Next, he would cut my heart out of my chest.

I picked up the parcel, took it to the rubbish bin in the corridor, then went out to the balcony for a cigarette. From there, I could see all the way to the railway station. Standing in front of the main entrance was a figure dressed in black, puffing on a cigarette and furtively glancing around.

The figure turned to look at me.

I quickly looked away, stubbed out my cigarette and ran back inside.

# Kerttu

The sun beat down from a cloudless sky as I drove towards Pasila police station. The heat made me long for the grey of October again. I know, I'm a bit weird, but in the grim autumn, no one thinks anything of it if I want to barricade myself in at home and watch television all day. Summer is different: every Finn is expected to burst with happiness simply because the sun is shining.

Koivuvyö was walking towards me in the lobby.

'You're up early. Don't work yourself to death!'

I had made it clear to Koivuvyö more than once that he could mock me to his heart's content outside of work. But on the job, he had to behave professionally. I felt like a priest, delivering a frustrated sermon to a congregation I knew wasn't listening.

'Remember, I'm your superior!'

Koivuvyö burst out laughing.

'I, Chief Inspector Koivuvyö, promise to obey you, Detective Superintendent Leppänen! If I break my word, may the devil take me!'

My blood boiled, and I wanted nothing more than to wipe the grin off his face. But before I could do anything, I found myself lying on the beach, basking in the sun and enjoying the quiet, broken only by the sound of the waves. I'd practised this exercise so many times that the image came to me almost automatically.

When the occupational health psychologist had recommended this technique to me last year, I'd dismissed it as utter nonsense. I would never have sought out a psychologist on my own, but Tiilihella had sent me there to deal with my anger management issues.

Koivuvyö was still in front of me, grinning. I couldn't rein him in—only Tiilihella could do that—but under no circumstances did I want to involve my boss in the mess between me and Koivuvyö. I'd made that mistake once already. Let him taunt me. Nothing would frustrate him more than if I refused to be provoked.

I stepped into the lift, satisfied that I had come up with a new strategy to wear him down.

Once I reached my office, I opened the safe. The lab technician had packed the evidence in protective plastic.

I noticed that my hands were covered in paint stains. The previous night, I had been finishing an abstract painting of fractal patterns in all different shades of red. I had no choice but to wash my hands and scrub the paint off. Eventually, I got them clean enough to pull on a pair of nitrile gloves.

I took the parcel from the safe.

I flinched.

The plastic covering had given me an electric shock. I took the scissors from my desk. My hands refused to cooperate.

I couldn't cut the plastic open and take out the diary.

As though I already knew that by opening that diary, I would unleash all the demons within it.

# Arto

The sender had left their teeth marks on the deathly white letter. There was nothing written on either side of the paper and no name on the envelope. I didn't even want to know what message they were trying to send.

You might think the letter would have shocked me, but I'd seen far worse. People sent Ida such shocking letters that no father would have let his daughter see them.

Ida might have known I'd started checking her room every morning for any sharp objects. But she had no idea I went through her post too.

I know, it's a crime to open other people's post, but in this case the end justified the means.

So far, I'd only given the letter paper and the envelope a cursory glance, but I wasn't going to let the sender off that easily! On my desk was a pile of letters and postcards that I intended to examine so carefully that I didn't miss a single detail. This ritual took up to an hour every evening, so closely did I scrutinize every envelope, right down to the folds of the paper.

I examined the envelope and the letter inch by inch with a magnifying glass, but I couldn't find fingerprints or any of the glue-like stains that I sometimes came across on the paper. The first time I'd seen a stain like that on an innocent-looking sheet of pink paper, I'd wracked my brains to think what on earth it could be. Eventually, it had dawned on me.

On that occasion, I didn't make it to the bathroom in time before throwing up on the floor in the hallway.

The stain on the letter was probably semen.

I had a system for sorting the dross we were sent into three categories. Messages from paedophiles who got off on stories about the horrific things Ida had experienced. I had nightmares about their sick fantasies. In my mind, Ida's real experiences at the hands of the Bastard intertwined with these sickos' wet dreams, and when I woke up, at first, I couldn't remember what my daughter had really been through in her torturer's clutches.

Letters asking Ida to give an interview, to be a guest on a podcast or to appear at a true-crime event. I knew she always turned down such invitations in no uncertain terms, so I didn't feel any pangs of guilt at keeping them from her.

Then there were letters and parcels containing all kinds of items related one way or another to Ida's case. Sometimes they had nothing to do with it:

An old scrapbook containing all the coverage in *Helsinki Today*.

A rusty old key that might be an allusion to the basement or the cage where Pekka Virtanen had imprisoned her. I hoped with all my heart that nobody had been locked away with the key sent to Ida.

A violet feather, the kind that kids glue to their Easter Witch costumes. Hard as I tried, I couldn't work out what this had to do with Ida's experiences.

There can't have been many people who were thrilled that the Post Office was such a mess these days. Sometimes it took months for letters to arrive, if they arrived at all, including some of those sent to Ida. In those cases, their aggressive tone didn't feel quite as distressing, because I imagined that whoever sent it had probably already got over their fit of rage and didn't even remember sending the letter.

Some stalkers started sending Ida letters as soon as the case against Clarissa and Pekka Virtanen began. When I opened those first letters, I called Ida's lawyer and asked whether I should report them to the police.

'No. Only contact the police when she starts to receive death threats.'

'When? Not if?'

'When,' the lawyer assured me.

Sometimes Ida got home before me. At these times, she opened her letters by herself. At least then, there was no post waiting on the floor in the hallway when I got home.

That day, I'd hurried home before her so that I could hide the post before she got back. Another assortment of letters and postcards was waiting on the worn brown mat in the porch.

I'd gone through the pile of post at my desk, torn open the envelopes, read all the letters and postcards. Nothing new, just more hate, craziness, more people sticking their noses in. The world in a microcosm.

Out of habit, I neatly organized the post into its respective folders.

As if, this way, I could keep the senders away from her.

# Ida

Visalahti appeared in front of me out of nowhere. He cut such a wily figure that he looked like the kind of second-hand car salesman you might see in a comedy sketch: there was nothing genuine in his broad smile, and not much in his laugh either.

Very deliberately, he steered me out to the balcony. I didn't even try to resist.

The balcony didn't have glass windows but a set of bars. Visalahti leant against them. Rust floated to the floor.

The paper's editorial office was situated on the tenth floor of a skyscraper. I felt dizzy at the mere thought of how high up we were. Whenever I came out here for a cigarette, I always tried to stand as close to the door as possible. I wouldn't have dreamt of peering over the railing.

The editor-in-chief seemed amused at my predicament. He chortled, but his laugh soon descended into a chesty smoker's cough.

He wanted to tell me his suggestion one on one. He didn't want my dad to hear what this was about. My dad and I didn't have any secrets… well, okay then… we did… plenty. But even after pondering for a moment, I couldn't think of anything that I wouldn't want Visalahti to say in front of my dad.

The editor fished two small cigars out of his jacket pocket. He offered one to me, then lit them both. According to Freud, sometimes a cigar is just a cigar, but to Visalahti it was a status symbol. It told me I was nothing but a poxy intern. He had all the power.

We puffed on our cigars in silence. Finally, he told me what this was all about, as though similar conversations were taking place at workplaces across the country.

I knew I'd never be able to think of him in the same way ever again.

I hadn't even noticed I'd clenched my fingers into a fist until blood started to ooze from my hand. The tiny spikes around the ring on my middle finger had pressed into my palm with such force that they had pierced the skin.

It seemed Visalahti was trying to keep me calm, which only made his proposal sound all the more unpleasant.

'I know you'd prefer to decline. But think about it from my perspective for a moment.'

I thought I already *had* declined. Maybe I hadn't managed to say no loud enough. I tried again. My vocal cords refused to cooperate.

'Don't think I suggest this sort of thing to all our interns. I don't. Ida, I know you well enough that I can trust you.'

Visalahti didn't appear to notice that I couldn't get a word out. He kept coming up with new arguments. I imagined him spending the previous night alongside his sleeping wife, writing down arguments in the little black book that he always carried around in his jacket pocket.

'This is just one way to advance your career. You'll soon realize it isn't that bad after all.'

I didn't want to hear any more.

'But remember one thing: don't tell your father anything about it. Mind you, Arto is old-school too; he's been round the block once or twice. He'd understand.'

'Fuck me,' I heard myself say.

Did he really think my dad would understand his proposition?

Visalahti's lips twisted themselves into a smile.

'Ida, I'm just thinking about what's best for you.'

The bars started shimmering in front of me. I didn't think I'd be able to put my delusions behind me. Of course, there weren't any actual bars on the railing around the balcony, but I still saw them.

I slipped a hand down my collar. I'd bought the key from an old bric-a-brac shop. It reminded me that I hadn't been locked in that cage forever. That I'd managed to escape. That I was free.

I pushed past Visalahti and ran along the corridor and back to the office and my desk. He called after me. I didn't stop.

I started packing my things into a box. My desk drawer was full of all the office equipment I'd hoarded like a magpie. I rummaged through the junk to find my personal belongings.

What childish dreams I'd been harbouring! That my internship might lead to a temporary position, the temporary position to a full-time job. That I might one day become a real reporter. What a joke!

My eyes finally stopped at the Barbamama pencil sharpener my mum had given me when I was a child and that I'd brought from home. I snatched it from the drawer and slipped it into the side pocket of my bag.

I stopped on the spot.

Visalahti wasn't going to win this game, not as long as I didn't give in to him. I hadn't achieved anything that I could be proud of in my life, but now a sense of self-respect, that I didn't even know I had, had started to take over.

Never again would I let a man wipe his grubby hands on me the way the Bastard did. That man wanted to destroy me. As soon as he'd arrived at the Niuvanniemi psychiatric hospital, he'd sent me a letter containing just one line:

*You are mine.*

Once I'd read the letter, I realized something. My life was all I had, but I was going to hold onto it with all my strength.

I'd attempted suicide a total of three times. After receiving that letter, I decided I wouldn't try a fourth time.

Visalahti knew he couldn't force me. I might hear a lot of insinuations. He might even repeat his request at some later date. But he could not sack me, not even if I disobeyed him.

But what would happen when I got sick of writing five-line news items? Then I might not have any choice but to reconsider Visalahti's suggestion.

# Kerttu

I stared at the diary as though wishing it would start talking to me. I didn't know where to begin. Should I read the book from start to finish or flick through it first, reading bits here and there?

This was the first time in Finnish criminal history that the police had got their hands on a serial killer's diary.

Eventually, I plucked up the courage to open the protective plastic. Initially, I decided to concentrate on the cover. I wished I could feel the sparkling glitter and the golden heart-shaped sequins with my bare hands.

And the sweet picture of an angel.

Along the upper edge of the cover were the words: *Dear Diary*. It reminded me of my own childhood diaries, where I had faithfully written every day's events, and every week I was in love with a different boy.

Why did a grown man want to describe the axe murder he had committed in a diary designed for little girls?

What if Koivuvyö had accidentally brought me a child's diary?

But when I opened the cover, I knew right away that this diary really did belong to a serial killer.

Even through my plastic gloves, I could feel how thin the paper was—cheap and bad quality, like something from the Soviet Union. The paper had sucked up the ink so much that it had soaked through to the other side, making it hard to read the text.

There were splodges here and there too, so the pages were smudged like an ink-blot test. The writer had tried to wipe some of the spots away and had only succeeded in defacing an entire page, making the text completely illegible.

The glitter on the cover rustled as I turned the pages. I held the diary closer to my nose and inhaled. It smelt of tobacco and apple-flavoured Hubba Bubba chewing gum. However, the diary's owner couldn't have been a hardened nicotine addict because the diary did not contain any nicotine-stained fingerprints. The strongest smell was Calvin Klein's trendy unisex fragrance One.

I didn't use perfume, but in my line of work I'd learnt to identify so many of them that my colleagues often invited me to the scene of a crime whenever the smell of perfume hung in the air. My sense of smell had solved a good few homicides over the years.

I took a magnifying glass from my desk and began examining the diary, comparing the texts on the different pages. The handwriting was the same.

The killer's handwriting was childish, like that of a little girl, curly and ornate. The cross on the 'T' dashed up towards the sky. The 'S' resembled a snake standing on end. Instead of dots on the 'I's, the killer had drawn little hearts.

Almost every sentence ended in an exclamation mark, as though the author had been unable to decide what was important and what was not. Even the most banal events (*It rained this afternoon! The rain stopped later in the afternoon!*) seemed to hold special significance. The sentence structures were simple and the writer's vocabulary very limited. There weren't any fancy terms in the text. Still, the writer had a firm command of grammar, and there were very few spelling mistakes.

A couple of pages had been torn out, rendering some sentences incomplete. Some pages had the same sentence written many times over (*He is dead! He is dead! He is dead!*). Some sentences, meanwhile, had been crossed out with the same pen (*Nobody can ever forgive me*).

One sentence appeared twenty-seven times, the writer repeating it like a mantra:

*I will finish the task I've been given.*

Did the killer perhaps have an accomplice deciding whom he should kill? Or was the killer suffering from some kind of psychotic breakdown and receiving instructions from God? My instinct told me that the killer was acting alone, though at the time I couldn't have said why I felt that way.

I wrote down my first impressions in my notebook. The killer was a neurotic control freak. He did not make mistakes. He had left the diary at the scene of the crime on purpose. The diary was bait, a lure that the killer hoped I would bite.

That must have been it. But it didn't make any sense. In my whole career, I'd never known a culprit to deliberately leave anything behind. Criminals didn't usually want to communicate with the police by leaving them a calling card, whether that was in the form of white roses in a vase, an embroidered handkerchief or a copy of *Thus Spake Zarathustra*.

We police officers talk about clues because it gives the impression that these are things we have discovered at the scene of a crime all by ourselves. More often than not, these clues are simply the criminal's mistakes. A carelessly wiped fingerprint on a door handle, a hair fallen on a pillow or a drop of blood from a cut finger: these are what lead the police to the culprit. Criminals only leave the police messages in detective stories.

I closed the diary, stood up and walked to the window. For a moment, I gazed up at the clouds floating across the sky. I tried to empty my mind so I could examine the diary again with fresh eyes. I wanted to find something new, something I might have missed the first time round.

I stroked the cover of the diary. One of the sequins cut a hole in my glove, and my fingertip poked through. I pulled off the glove, threw it in the bin and pulled on another one. I began reading the diary from the beginning once again.

*I won't stop until they're all dead. Their lives are in my hands.*

The killer knew who he was going to kill next.

I'm not sure what I was thinking the first time I'd picked up the diary. That the killer would confess to everything? That he would swear never to do it again?

This time I wasn't answerable only to the police service, my subordinates or the Finnish people. I was answerable to *them*, the people the killer was referring to in the diary: *Their lives are in my hands.*

I took a tattered old envelope from my desk drawer, removed a photograph and looked the figure right in the eyes.

I couldn't stand seeing that face again, so I hurriedly slid the photograph back into the envelope, put it back in the drawer and hid it under a pile of papers.

# Arto

Ida was lazily twiddling her spoon in her spinach soup. I didn't have a clue what she was thinking. But she certainly wasn't going to taste her lunch.

At home, we did our best to avoid each other, like two freshers that bureaucracy had randomly housed in the same digs who didn't know each other and had no intention of doing so. But at work there was no avoiding each other; if nothing else, then at least in order to show our colleagues that we were on excellent terms, that our father–daughter relationship was warm and close.

The first time I'd heard about Ida's devastating suffering was when she testified against her tormentors in court. We had never spoken about Clarissa or the Bastard, not even during the trial. I knew everything that had happened to Ida, though she herself hadn't told me anything.

At long last, I now had the opportunity to be a proper father to her, but my thoughts were elsewhere. I'd been stupid enough to believe that the wall of silence between us couldn't possibly get any taller, but I was gravely mistaken.

We were sitting in the *Helsinki Today* staff canteen on the ground floor of the glass tower. I knew that we would again be able to enjoy our lunch together, just the two of us, though there was room at the table for four others. Our colleagues were always painfully polite, but the truth was they didn't want to have anything to do with us.

I didn't blame them.

Bad luck isn't contagious, but still, it's best not to take the risk.

Besides, from the moment she and I had started working at the newspaper, it was obvious that our colleagues didn't have a clue what to say to us. When we meet someone who is grieving a loved one, we resort to a few set phrases. Some people made the mistake of saying such things to me too, though despite everything she'd been through, my daughter was still alive.

After Ida had moved back in with me, I'd tried to stimulate her appetite by taking her to gourmet restaurants and by cooking her favourite childhood foods, but it was pointless. I decided not to stick my nose into her eating habits any more, but it was hard. Now, as my eyes followed her spoon, she probably thought I was judging her.

The silence between us continued; it seemed to be screaming in my ears, though the canteen was full of life: our colleagues were chatting loudly, laughing at one another's jokes.

A fly landed on the edge of Ida's plate. I glanced at the nearest window and noticed that it was ajar. Ida seemed pleased; now she had a valid excuse not to eat her food. She dropped her spoon into the bowl. Soup splashed onto the tablecloth. I took the drab brown napkin from my tray and wiped the splashes of soup away.

The beep of a text message interrupted my train of thought. I took out my phone, but I hadn't received anything. Ida rummaged in her bag for her phone.

Something flashed across her eyes as she read the message, something I hadn't dared imagine I'd ever seen again.

A glimmer of joy.

Something flickered inside me. Ida had someone important, someone special!

I looked at her, and it felt like I was witnessing something private, something not intended for my eyes. I forced myself to look away and to stare at the window instead. The sun shone right in my face and I squinted, trying my hardest not to show how excited I was.

'Seems like you've got a secret admirer,' I said, aiming for a cheerful tone.

Ida seemed tongue-tied. My intuition was right. She avoided eye contact and started scratching at her cuticles. After a moment, she managed to spit it out.

'It's just someone I met.'

I'll never forget how lonely Ida was before we moved in together; how she used to pace up and down in her apartment, cut off from the rest of the world. But now I wasn't her only social contact. Hope began to raise its head like the first crocus in spring.

It seemed I wasn't going to get any more out of her, but I couldn't help myself, I had to try.

'Are you dating?'

There was a little too much hope in my voice, perhaps even desperation. Ida gave a deep sigh as though she was about to tell me what was going on, to tell me everything. But eventually, all she said was:

'We've only met once.'

I pictured myself standing proudly beside her at the magistrates and watching her and her partner joined in wedlock. I told myself to relax, but I couldn't rein in my imagination.

Besides, why shouldn't I be excited? I'd missed out on everything that fathers usually experience. No postcards from an exchange trip to Buenos Aires or New York, no Interrailing around Europe, no high-school graduation, no university place. Even moving into her own apartment had been a disaster. She had retreated into her bedsit to die, alone, like an animal sensing its fate.

My colleagues' children were all married; they had kids of their own, some had several. To these colleagues, it was a given that everything would work out in their children's lives. They took for granted all the things I had been denied.

I felt like standing up and shouting at the top of my lungs, extolling my happiness to everyone in the canteen.

*My daughter has a boyfriend!* Or should I say, a gentleman friend? She was an adult, after all. Perhaps it was a girlfriend—a lady friend; I didn't care either way. What was most important was that there was somebody who loved her, and that she had finally found someone to love back.

In any case, I was going to become a grandfather! I realized that my dreams had died long ago, fizzled out over time, so slowly that I'd barely noticed it. Ida had been so sick, and I was certain that the sickness had left her sterile, that she would never have children of her own. But miracles can happen!

'Arto, have you ever wondered about how little attention these five-line murder stories get?'

Ida changed the subject awkwardly. She clearly didn't want to talk about her lover. I gave in but hoped she would talk about her romance later, when she was ready.

I found it hard to concentrate on what she was saying. Arto—of course! Arto. Not *Dad.* That's how distant we were.

The answer to her question was no. Sometimes my subconscious managed to conjure up the notion that it could have been me lying in a ditch instead of the deceased, but I quickly pushed the idea back where it had come from.

'Now that we've been writing about these deaths, they've started to interest me more than those that get all the attention,' she said.

To be perfectly honest, the subject didn't interest me in the least. The reason these banal deaths didn't get any more column space was precisely because nobody was interested in them. That was the obvious explanation. Death was inevitable. Junkies had a habit of overdosing and dying. Alcoholics sometimes fell over and hit their head. Unlike the deaths that people talked about for years, sometimes even decades, with these five-line stories there was nothing out of the ordinary, nothing to say.

I realized that Ida had given the matter a great deal of thought. She furrowed her brow and rubbed her temples, as though the severity of the subject made her head throb with pain. Though I felt largely indifferent about the topic, I was grateful that Ida had struck up conversation with me, no matter how trivial the subject.

'What if some of those deaths weren't accidents after all? What if one of them was a murder? The police probably don't put many resources into investigating the deaths of people living on the margins of society.'

She chuckled. 'I want to believe.'

*The X Files* had always been her favourite TV show. But, at least at that moment, I wasn't quite ready to believe.

And it was then that Ida told me her idea. She wanted us to start investigating these five-line deaths.

I nearly rejected the idea out of hand. But there was something in her eyes, something I didn't realize at the time was so significant but that I had a burning desire to understand.

Nothing was more important to me than understanding Ida. And I hadn't done anything to make it happen. And that's why I agreed.

Who knows? Maybe it was fate, deciding on my behalf.

At least, I hoped I'd be able to blame something other than myself.

I can recall the sight of us sitting there opposite each other in the staff canteen that smelt of spinach soup.

And I wanted to shout: 'Don't do it!'

# Ida

Blood stained the cobblestones of Hakaniemi Square around my victim's head. His expression was calm. From the man's face, there was no way of knowing how he had met his end only a moment ago.

I'd struck up conversation with a homeless tramp and asked for a swig from his bottle. He'd been sitting on a bench by himself at the edge of the otherwise empty square, enjoying a gulp from a half-empty bottle of vodka. He'd refused to share it with me, so I'd ripped it from his hands. After a short tussle, I'd knocked him off the bench. He hit his head against the cobblestones. Fatally.

I was convinced the police wouldn't think this was murder.

But a disturbing thought suddenly started to form in my mind.

My victim had got off too easily.

A quick knock, and now he was dead. This murder was so wishy-washy that I was almost embarrassed. To settle for such a limp little shove.

An old drunk or a bunch of teenagers would have made just as much of a mess of this one. I was ashamed of not being able to carry out my task with honour. The nagging dissatisfaction gradually turned into weary frustration. Luckily, there hadn't been anybody around to witness my complete and utter failure.

Was it possible to improve a murder retroactively? It looked like this one had been carried out by a bungling amateur. My victim was already dead; there was nothing I could do about that. But could I make the death look more violent than was actually the case, but in such a way that the police didn't start investigating it as a homicide?

I crouched over the body, tried to grab hold of his tangled mullet, but his hair was so wet with blood that I couldn't get a firm grip.

I let his hair go and took hold of his left ear instead. I lifted his head, then smashed it down against the cobblestones. His skull gave a satisfying pop, like cracking an enormous egg. Now the body looked properly roughed up, but the police would still probably think this was an accident and not a murder.

Only then did I notice that the pool of blood around the victim's head looked like a butterfly.

Four years ago, I'd murdered the former finance minister Uolevi Mäkisarja. When he died, I'd noticed a bloody stain on his bedroom rug. After examining the stain, I came the conclusion that there was a butterfly in front of me.

At the time, I'd tried to convince myself that I could stop killing, but I'd burst out laughing before I'd even thought it through properly.

The body lying on the cobblestones was proof that I hadn't stopped. And I never would. Not as long as I could avoid getting caught.

I was a serial killer. And proud of it.

# Kerttu

I took off my nitrile gloves and threw them in the wastepaper basket. I wished I could have thrown away all the thoughts I'd had throughout the day with them, thoughts so jumbled that even I couldn't make sense of them, but I knew it was futile. My mind would not rest until this killer was put away.

I decided to go home. In the car park, the evening sunshine glared mercilessly. I'd left my sunglasses on my desk.

Just as I was preparing to go back and get them, something caught my attention.

There was a man sitting in my car.

I took out my weapon, headed towards the door on the driver's side, slowly creeping closer to the car.

The sun disappeared behind a cloud.

The seat was empty.

I put my pistol back in its holder.

I could no longer touch my weapon without thinking about the bullet I had fired a year earlier.

I pressed my hands against the car and kept them there until they stopped trembling.

In my mind's eye, I could see the faces of all the men at whose hands I could have died.

And nearly did.

Some of the situations were surprising, some not so much. In call-outs from the emergency services where a man is threatening to kill his wife, a police officer can easily end up becoming the victim, especially a female one. Anything can happen when gangs decide to settle their differences. Even junkies can be unpredictable.

But worst of all were the cases I called 'tails': the stalkers.

At the present time, I didn't have any tails, because all my recent stalkers had been caught, albeit not for harassing me but for other crimes: armed robbery or murder. Of course, there could have been someone else following me. Sometimes I didn't find out about the stalkers until after they had been caught.

One of my tails, who had just been banged up, had been stalking me for years. He followed my female colleagues too, because, according to him, *being a cop is no job for a woman*. Or so he told me in the Christmas card accompanying a parcel of faeces that he once posted through my door.

Apart from the parcel, this tail had never contacted me directly. I'd lulled myself into thinking he was probably harmless, although I knew I shouldn't think like that. A false sense of security has killed many women in similar situations. This is why people should always take stalkers seriously.

However, another of my tails had caused me so much distress that I'd thought of little else. This one had a habit of sending me death threats. I'd managed to put my fear and anxiety to one side while the messages were sent to my work address. But when letters started arriving on my windscreen while my car was parked outside my own house, I could no longer make light of the situation; so I went to a hotel for a few nights to escape the threats.

I started to look for my car keys in my handbag but couldn't find them. I took everything out one item at a time and placed them on the bonnet. My lipstick fell to the ground and rolled under the car.

There were no bombs attached the underside of my car.

This time.

Olavi Seittilä had gone to prison because of a mistake I had made. I'd been convinced that he had murdered his wife. Nonetheless, Seittilä was released from prison once the real killer confessed after being caught for a second homicide. The damages awarded to Seittilä by the state could never compensate for the years he had spent in prison and did nothing to alleviate my guilt. Many years had passed since his release, but he still sent me threatening letters. Once, he had even placed a bomb under my car. I decided not to report him to the police. I deserved his hatred.

I gathered my things and put them back in my handbag. The keys were not among them. I swore out loud, and only then noticed the bulge in my blouse pocket and remembered I'd put them there because I had been in a hurry this morning.

When I got home, I sat down on the couch, closed my eyes and heard a voice in my head.

*Each time a flea bites you, think of me.*

My best friend Esko had written this little note in my diary when we were children. Why had this nursery rhyme that I hadn't heard for years suddenly popped into my head?

Of course!

The serial killer's diary.

If only its glittery covers had contained the sweet rhymes of an innocent child and not the fantasies of a twisted mind, fantasies that the killer had made come true.

I mentally ran through all the observations that I had made

while examining the diary. None of them moved my investigation forwards. I was still at square one.

When I stood up, I noticed that the floor looked like it had been raining hailstones. While thinking about the case, I'd barely noticed that I was tearing tissue after tissue into thin strips then rolling them into tiny balls. The box was almost empty. As though I was a witch enacting an age-old ritual to catch this killer once and for all.

Or kill him.

The diary had been in the lab for far too long, though I'd been absolutely sure—and I was right—that examining it with laboratory techniques would be pointless. The diary hadn't provided any bodily fluids—sperm, blood, mucus, sweat, urine or faeces—or any fibres and only a few smudged fingerprints. And why would it? The killer hadn't left any traces at the crime scene either.

I was hopelessly late. The killer had a head start.

Suddenly a curious thought entered my mind.

I wasn't hunting the killer. The killer was hunting me.

# Ida

From my desk drawer I took a scrapbook where I'd started collecting all the pieces I'd written for *Helsinki Today*. I'd spent almost an hour in the bookshop going through different notebooks and folders until I found the one I wanted. This one had twenty pages made of thick card, and I could buy more if I needed them. The folder was covered with purple velvet that tickled the skin of my palm like fresh moss. I imagined the folder slowly filling with work.

I opened *Helsinki Today*, cut out the article I'd written and glued it into the scrapbook.

*Body found in Hakaniemi Square.*

The article revealed that a market trader had discovered a man's lifeless body in the early hours of the morning. The berry seller had identified the deceased as a homeless man who slept on the streets around the market.

I could see the man's chapped face. It wasn't hard to imagine his appearance. Human wrecks like him were constantly traipsing through the streets of Helsinki. His blood-shot eyes had sunk deep into their sockets. His nose and cheeks were red like Father Christmas's. His face was framed with wispy grey hair: a tangled mop that turned to limp sideburns around the ears and a straggly stubble on his chin.

His death had merited exactly five lines of text in *Helsinki Today*. Wasn't his life worth more than this? Apparently not.

And what if it wasn't just the editor that thought this but the police too? What if they weren't taking the investigation into his death seriously? What if the coroner had simply measured his blood-alcohol levels, and that was it? Case closed. The police were always complaining about a lack of funding, but surely they couldn't cut corners when it came to investigating a cause of death.

I found myself walking around my desk, quietly muttering to myself. I could sense a thought taking shape in my mind, but I couldn't quite make it out yet. I stopped, read the piece again.

Drug addicts in the rough Kallio neighbourhood. Tramps hanging around the train station. Drunks sitting by the shore at Tokoinranta.

When I had read *Helsinki Today* in the past, I had skipped over the news of their deaths too. They were just column filler, like characters dying in a video game, where the only thing that mattered was killing as many of them as possible. The only people interested in them were sociologists pondering societal problems on the evening news. And statisticians who calculated the total number of the deaths in the previous year.

These deaths often happened without the families ever missing the deceased, though they might not have seen their relative for weeks, months or even years. When the police eventually rang the family's doorbell, the news never came as a surprise. Mentally, they had bidden farewell to their loved ones long ago.

The families' attitude felt heartless, but at the end of the day I understood them. They had probably hoped beyond hope that their alcoholic sister would kick the booze or that their heroin-addict son would finally go clean. But eventually their loved ones had slipped out of reach. They had realized that they would be unable to live their own lives if they spent all their time waiting for a miracle. And so, in their minds, they had already severed the last thin thread holding them together.

*How easy it would be to murder someone that nobody will miss!*

I had a strange feeling.

Almost as if it wasn't my own thought at all.

Almost as though someone had planted it in my mind.

An image started to take shape in my mind, and I tried to erase it as soon as it had appeared.

I didn't want to confront the truth.

I still don't want to, but by now I don't have any other option.

# Kerttu

The victim's front door was still cordoned off with police tape bearing the official command, POLICE AREA DO NOT CROSS, in both Finnish and Swedish. I took the key out of my handbag and lifted the tape out of the way.

Normally I spent Saturdays at work. This time, however, I hadn't gone to the office but had come to the scene of the crime, the place where we had found the serial killer's diary.

The initial investigation had been concluded. Whenever possible, physical evidence should be collected within forty-eight hours of the crime. However, the investigators still hadn't informed the victim's family that the investigation was over. My subordinates knew that I always wanted to give the crime scene a thorough going-over one last time.

Everything looked familiar. The stylish living room, dominated by an enormous sofa. The cosy kitchen with a slice of stale strawberry cream cake still on a plate on the table. The tastefully decorated bedroom where the victim had been killed with an axe.

I have a photographic memory. Many times, I've made my subordinates' jaws drop when after visiting a scene only once, I'm still able to describe it down to the last detail. And so, coming here now for the second time, I felt as though I had been here countless times before.

I could have played the game that Esko and I used to play as children. Someone could have pulled a giant sheet over the crime scene and removed one item of furniture from underneath it. When the sheet was lifted away, I would have known right away what was missing.

I stopped, lost in thought, standing next to the bed, on the exact same spot that the killer would have stood.

'You have to get inside the killer's head! What was he feeling? What was he thinking? If you can't answer these two questions, you'll never crack the case.'

Heiskanen, an instructor at the police academy, had repeated these questions so often that I could still hear his voice.

While investigating my first cases, I would fly into a panic when I realized I hadn't the faintest idea how to answer Heiskanen's questions. What had the killer been thinking in one of my first cases when he had killed a man with a fileting knife in a dark alley, though we had also found a pistol at the scene?

It took years before I realized that we police officers each have our own way of solving crimes, and none of them is more right or wrong than the others.

I approached crimes from a different angle from Heiskanen, but we got the same results.

I was less interested in the murderer and more interested in the victim. If I could dive into the victim's mind and work out what they were thinking and feeling, then I would get to the bottom of the case.

I will never forget the time when Heiskanen had placed a selection of photographs on a table in front of us students. They were photos of victims whose cases had never been solved. After he had laid out the photographs like a grim game of Patience, he watched our reactions. Then, with one swipe of the hand, he cast the photographs onto the floor and told me to leave the room. Out in the corridor, I took a tissue from my handbag and dried the corners of my eyes.

At that moment I realized that, if I ever wanted to succeed in my career, to progress from a police constable to sergeant (as a woman, it had been clear that my career would go no further than that), I had to pretend, as convincingly as possible, that I had no emotions. Nothing moved me, neither brutalized bodies nor relatives weeping in agony.

Every single day, I would have to prove to the others—and to myself—that a woman *can* be a police officer. I mustn't be timid, sensitive, motherly or warm. Heiskanen never said it directly, but he insinuated that for a police officer the greatest virtue is aggression. When we practised arresting people, some of the boys were a little too rough with the handcuffs, leaving the others with bruises. But Heiskanen always turned a blind eye: in real-life situations, these boys will have to deal with the hardest of hardened criminals.

From my handbag I took my wallet, and from there the photograph of the victim.

I looked him in the eye and repeated the promise I'd made the first time I'd visited this scene. The same promise I'd given every victim whose murder I'd investigated: 'I will catch your killer.'

Luckily, it was a promise I'd mostly been able to keep. But naturally I didn't remember those cases. I only remembered my failures. I'd learnt something every time.

If nothing else, then at least that people are only too happy to make the same mistakes more than once.

I walked around the apartment one last time. The bedroom. The kitchen, The living room. Suddenly, I noticed a piece of scrunched-up paper on the small Chippendale coffee table. I raised my gloved hand, picked it up and straightened it out.

Drawn on the paper was a set of gallows. The game was only just starting, and only two letters had been added to the puzzle. 'A' was both the first and the last letter of this eight-letter word. Underneath the gaps were two letters that had been crossed out: 'Y' and 'N'. Incorrect answers.

Who had the victim been playing with? His killer? Had he guessed he would soon be as lifeless as the stick man hanging from the gallows as the game progressed?

Either my subordinates hadn't noticed this piece of paper or, which I thought more likely because I trusted their attention to detail, they didn't think it was suspicious, and that's why they hadn't bagged it and put it in evidence.

They were probably right; it probably wasn't of any value. Perhaps the victim had simply amused himself with a game of Hangman.

Still, just in case, I took an evidence bag out of my pocket, pushed the scrap of paper inside and put the bag in my backpack.

I was about to leave the apartment when something glinted on the floor in the hallway. I crouched down to look at it more closely.

A small heart-shaped sequin glimmered in the light. The same kind of sequin that had been on the cover of the killer's diary. I picked it up and clenched it in my fist.

Once in the car park, I opened my fist, looked at the sequin for a moment, then blew it into the air and watched as the wind caught it and whirled it around vigorously.

I said my wish out loud, as if I'd seen a shooting star.

If I had told Tiilihella right then that I had no intention of continuing with the investigation, despite his orders, everything might have turned out differently.

But I doggedly carried on, heading towards my own destruction.

# Ida

I drew the outlines of the body on the cobblestones as best I could imagine. I had to kneel in order to reach under the bench. The line I was sketching in blood-red chalk kept breaking as if it had been drawn by an old, quivering hand.

Passers-by looked at me in confusion. Some of them even pointed at me. I didn't know if it was because I was Ida the Psycho Shrink Survivor or because I was curled up under a bench inside the contours I'd drawn.

The body had been discovered last week. I hadn't seen any information about what position it was in when it was found, only that it had been found under the bench. So, I had to use my imagination. I didn't want to ask the police or rely on them.

Sunlight filtered through the bench's narrow planks. I felt safe, as though I was sheltered inside the outlines, untouchable, just like when I was a child and I played hide-and-seek with my dad. I'd hidden in my mother's wardrobe, in among her colourful dresses and tunics and pretended to be invisible.

I thought only of the body. And of how it had become a body.

I'd snuck out halfway through an editorial meeting at *Helsinki Today*, because I wanted to examine the location in peace, without my dad. He had remained in the conference room, and nobody noticed me slipping out. My contribution to the paper was pretty small.

A terrifying thought had consumed me.

What if the homeless guy really had been murdered?

According to the police press release, he had passed out on the bench, fallen to the ground and struck his head against the cobbles.

Something wasn't right.

I crawled out from under the bench, then lay down on it. Flakes of poisonous-green paint came loose and scratched my hands. If he had fallen from the bench, there was no way he could have ended up underneath it. He must have fallen in front of the bench, then crawled underneath it to hide. But hide from what? If nobody had pushed him from the bench but he had fallen by accident as he passed out, then nobody had threatened him. So how could his body have been discovered *under* the bench?

What if my suspicions were right after all?

My phone felt hot in my pocket. Rather, the text message it contained radiated heat like a stove in a sauna. I took out my phone, read the message again. I still hadn't answered it. I wasn't sure whether the person who sent it was taking the piss. It couldn't have been serious. I refused even to consider the possibility.

I crammed myself under the bench again, curled up inside the contours I'd drawn.

I closed my eyes, imagined I was the body that had been discovered there. It was only a short fall from the bench to the ground, especially if the victim hadn't fallen from a sitting position but while lying on the bench. Could someone really die from such a short fall? Surely the head couldn't possibly have hit the cobbles hard enough to kill him.

It wasn't for me to question the cause of death that the coroner had determined, though little children are always falling from their stools or feeding chairs and they only end up with a bump on their head and before you know it, they're jumping up and down on the back of the sofa again.

I opened my eyes. My attention was drawn to the planks of the bench. Was I seeing wrong? No, someone had carved an image into one of the planks, maybe with a pocketknife. The marks were faint; I couldn't quite make them out. I decided to take a photograph of the bench.

All of a sudden, I noticed a pair of hairy legs walking towards me. Someone shoved their phone a little too close to my face. I tried to dodge it, but I had no chance. Snap.

*I'm not Ida the Psycho Shrink Survivor*, I wanted to shout. I was much more than that. I was me. I was more than what the Bastard had done to me. His actions didn't make me *me*; they hadn't shaped my personality, although, of course, they had. But I was me despite them, not because of them.

I knew I was going to have that familiar dream again: I'd be sitting in Clarissa's waiting room on a chair with a sheepskin draped over it. The warmth of the sheepskin would remind me of the previous patient, and that I wasn't Clarissa's only one. I'd flick through a foreign fashion magazine, the newest edition of *Vogue* or *Elle.* On the shining cover of the magazine, there would be a model, or maybe an actress or a singer I didn't recognize. I'd contemplate how little I had in common with other women, with people in general, how far I'd drifted from humanity.

Or maybe I'd be sitting opposite Clarissa in her surgery, listening to her fortune-cookie aphorisms: 'No soul should take on a burden beyond what it can bear.' The plastic diamonds glued to her fake nails would sparkle like droplets of blood. When I woke up in the morning, the first thing I would smell would be Chanel N°5, and I wouldn't be able to tell whether the dream had been real or not.

I'd wanted to take back control of my life, to reclaim it. But there was a stain on my forehead, one that I'd never be able to wash away.

The man who snapped a picture of me disappeared as quickly as he'd appeared. I hauled myself up from under the bench and patted away the dust and the dandelion seeds stuck to the back of my trousers.

I stood next to the bench a moment longer and wondered whether I'd conducted this forensic examination according to the rule book. Was there anything I'd forgotten? How had the police taken care of it?

Surely there was nothing to suggest this really was a murder. I was stroking the back of the bench, lost in thought, when suddenly something caught in my fingers.

A hair.

My heart started beating frantically.

The murderer's hair.

It might belong to the victim.

Or anyone who had sat on the bench. It could have been my hair. It probably was my hair. It was dyed jet black.

The police would surely have examined every inch of the bench and gathered all the available evidence. The hair must have become caught on the bench only after the police had finished their forensic examination. Nonetheless, I decided to take it with me. If I was going to play detective, I needed to play properly. I pressed the hair into my pocket.

My theory had more holes than a sieve. To be honest, it was one enormous abyss.

But I felt like I was finally getting a grip on something. I just didn't know what.

# Kerttu

The psychiatrist turned her back to me and walked to the window. She couldn't bring herself to look me in the eyes but glanced at me over her shoulder, as though she was afraid I might attack her.

'I—'

The psychiatrist turned so quickly and gave me such a piercing look that it cut my sentence short.

I hadn't thought about my encounter with the psychiatrist for decades. But now, as I took the pictures of angels decorated with sparkling glitter out of my handbag, I recalled trembling feverishly as I sat down in her leather armchair shortly after I'd graduated from high school.

Tiilihella knew nothing about my past. And neither did my subordinates.

At the police-academy entrance exams, the applicants were asked about any traumatic experiences that might affect their ability to discharge their duties. I had neglected to mention my own trauma.

Now I was sitting behind my desk admiring embossed pictures of angels. I had bought them at a stationer's that morning on my way to work; every time I stepped into that shop it felt like being whisked back to my childhood. My old friend Esko and I always used to go there to buy pictures, stickers and paper dolls.

I carefully started cutting one of the angels from the picture. He was leaning his head against his left arm, a pensive look on his face. The assistant must have thought these pictures were for my grandchildren and not that they would be used in the line of duty.

The picture shed glitter, which floated to my desk like stardust, as though I were leading a kindergarten craft session for a group of excitable children and not laying the groundwork for a deadly serious investigation into a serial killer.

As children, pictures of angels had definitely been our favourites, though Esko and I hadn't yet heard of Raphael or his painting of the *Sistine Madonna*.

The first time I saw Raphael's masterpiece was on the ceiling of the dentist's surgery when I was getting a filling. I was fifteen at the time. I recognized the angels from my pictures. As soon as the brutal procedure was over, I had walked to the stationer's and bought a reproduction of the painting. I attached it to the wall opposite my bed with Sellotape, so that the angels would be the last thing I saw when I closed my eyes and the first thing I saw when I opened them in the morning.

I decided that one day I would go and visit my dear angels in person.

On the last day of August, after my high-school graduation, the sun was shining in Dresden, clouds glided across the sky and a faint breeze caressed my face. A queue of tourists had formed outside the gates of the Gemäldegalerie Alte Meister.

The breeze lifted the hem of my lace dress just enough to cool my ankles. I imagined it was the nineteenth century, I was a princess, and the Zwinger Museum, where the gallery was housed, was my castle.

However, the buoyant atmosphere was dulled somewhat by my argument with Esko earlier that morning. He had driven me to the airport, hectoring me all the way.

'I don't know why you're giving in to your parents and applying to the police academy. Why don't you follow your dreams and study law?'

Esko hadn't realized that his ranting felt every bit as upsetting as my parents', and once I'd heard enough of his outburst, I'd made it abundantly clear to him.

When I finally arrived at the museum, I hurriedly looked around the works on display—the Rembrandts, the Botticellis and Titians—the classics speeding past my eyes. I couldn't even bring myself to stop and admire the soft contours of Giorgione's naked *Sleeping Venus* but quickened my step towards Raphael's cherubs.

When I reached the *Sistine Madonna*, a group of Japanese tourists had gathered in front of it, the same tourists that had been getting on my nerves in the queue outside. I arrived behind them just as their guide began leading them into the next room.

I stood in front of the Madonna, alone.

I turned to look at the faces of the angels at the lower edge of the painting. The left-hand angel's face was plump as a baby's, but I could not see the face of the right-hand one.

Now there was something else in its place.

Looking back at me from the painting was Esko.

Esko's face and the angel's face merged into one another like a painting done in watercolours that the artist hadn't allowed to dry in peace and whose colours had started to seep into one another.

Esko's sensitive, handsome, intelligent face.

My heels started to rise until eventually they no longer touched the floor.

I stood there on the balls of my feet until they too were only barely touching the ground.

I was floating in front of the painting.

The angels were flying around me, their laughter pealing out like bells.

The dazzlingly beautiful beings lifted me higher and higher until my head was touching the ceiling.

The floor felt so cold against my cheek that it gave me goosebumps.

My ears were ringing. I noticed there was blood trickling from my nose. My tights had ripped, leaving my knees bare. There was a pain in my right ankle. My mouth was dry, and my tongue felt rough.

Someone I did not know was sitting next to me on the floor, holding my hand. A group of people had gathered around us; people staring, pointing at me and muttering to one another. I didn't understand a word.

My mind was empty. I caught sight of a clock on the wall. It said it was two o'clock, but I wasn't sure whether it was two in the morning or two at night. I tried to remember who I was but couldn't even remember my name. My heart was trying to push its way out of my chest. I gazed across the room and, judging from the paintings, concluded I must be in an art gallery.

The person sitting next to me tried to let go of my hand. I clenched the hand tighter, because if I'd let go, I would have floated up to the ceiling again.

The person holding my hand was a museum security guard and asked me once more whether someone ought to call an ambulance. I couldn't answer the question because I had no idea what had happened or whether I needed help. Finally, the guard suggested calling a taxi so I could return to my hotel and rest.

The following morning, I awoke in my hotel room to my own screams. I was having a nightmare: the police had arrested me and taken me to a psychiatric hospital as soon as I'd returned to Finland. Once in the hospital, I'd been sectioned, locked up against my will and restrained in a straitjacket.

I decided to return home immediately and that, as soon as I got back, I would make an appointment with a psychiatrist. I called the airport and managed to change my ticket so I could fly home the very same day. I stood up and hurriedly began packing my belongings. I was in such a panic that it was only once I arrived home that I realized I had left the silver bracelet that Esko had given me as a graduation present on the bedside table in my hotel room.

On the bus to the airport, I glanced around, wondering whether the other passengers could tell I was in a psychotic state. The old woman sitting next to me peered at me from beneath her thick eyebrows. I suppose she thought she was being subtle, but I couldn't help noticing her looks.

I tried to think what I had done and, more importantly, what I had looked like back when I was still well. I couldn't even begin to comprehend that only yesterday, a mere twenty-four hours ago, I could have been sitting on this exact same bus on my way from the airport to the hotel, taking my health for granted.

I scrutinized a young woman sitting opposite me: her hands in her lap, her miniskirt, her slender legs demurely together. I tried to copy her, but my legs automatically wanted to be apart. I wiped the sweat from my brow and had to force myself to stay in the same position.

When the bus arrived at the airport, I watched a teenage girl walking in front of me and tried to imitate her. On the aeroplane, I didn't dare eat or drink anything. I felt nauseous. I asked the flight attendant for a blanket and curled up underneath it. For the rest of the flight, I pretended to be asleep.

As soon as the plane's wheels touched down with a bump on the runway, I barged my way to the front so I could get off first, as the other passengers looked on in disproval.

Once I got home, I dropped my suitcase to the floor, grabbed the phone and booked an appointment with a private psychiatrist.

I can still remember what it felt like sitting in the waiting room, all my hope thrown to the wind. Sweat poured down my back, but I tried to enjoy my last moments of freedom. I was sure I would soon find myself in the same place as in my dreams.

Finally, the door opened, and the psychiatrist called me into her office. There was a print on the wall behind her desk, the sensual *Sleeping Venus*—a woman lying naked with only her fingers covering her modesty—a painting that I'd hurried past on my way to Raphael's angels.

I had barely sat down in the armchair when I started telling the psychiatrist what had happened to me in the museum.

She listened to my story, sober and serious, and when I reached the end of my account, she stood up and walked to the window. I imagined she wanted to grant me another few moments of mercy before giving her verdict.

Eventually, she turned, but instead of returning to her chair, she walked to the bookshelf, searched for a moment, then took a thick book with a plain black cover from the shelf.

Judging by her age, I didn't imagine she would have to consult a book to find a suitable diagnosis for me, but it seemed I was mistaken.

She returned to her chair and leafed through the pages, muttering so quietly that I could not hear what she was saying. I craned my neck, and to my great surprise the book that the psychiatrist was flicking through was not a scientific opus but an art book. After another moment of leafing and muttering, she found what she was looking for and handed the book to me, her expression still deadly serious.

'So, you saw this masterpiece by Raphael?' she asked, pointing to the image of the *Sistine Madonna* on the right-hand page.

I gave an uncertain nod. Would the psychiatrist give me a different diagnosis if I hadn't lost my mind in front of the *Sistine Madonna* but one of Raphael's other paintings, a work depicting the Virgin Mary—the *Madonna del Granduca*, for instance?

'You are my first patient to suffer from Stendhal Syndrome.'

I'd never heard of such a thing. I imagined Stendhal must have been someone who had suffered from something similar and after whom the syndrome was named. The name didn't ring any bells because when I was younger, I wasn't interested in crosswords and hadn't constantly come across the common clue: French author, eight letters.

'Stendhal Syndrome is also known as Florence Syndrome.'

I nodded at the doctor as I tried to put the pieces of the puzzle together.

Soon she told me that, after coming down with the syndrome, Stendhal was locked away in a Florentine sanatorium where he eventually died, alone and forgotten. I found it hard to breathe, as though the oxygen in the room had suddenly evaporated.

But the doctor eventually put my mind at rest.

'You are perfectly healthy. Raphael simply caused you an overwhelming flood of emotions. Art affects us sensitive souls more than other people.'

The psychiatrist had given me a clean bill of health. I started to laugh hysterically. I couldn't believe that I'd been so worried—for nothing. It felt as though the laughter was bubbling out of me like lava from a volcano, and I was worried that it might never stop. The doctor seemed a little worried too, as she reached into the cupboard in her desk and took out a bottle of sedatives. I almost couldn't take the pills for all the laughing, but eventually managed to swallow them.

Back then, I still hadn't realized that I shouldn't trust my mind so readily.

# Arto

The bus was full. The teenage boy sitting next to me was chewing gum, blowing enormous bubbles and listening to hip hop so loud that his earbuds might as well have been in my ears and not his.

Across the aisle, someone's phone started to ring. A man in a stylish suit answered, then started shouting, as if the caller might not hear him otherwise. As soon as he stopped hollering into his phone, my own beeped as a message arrived. I was already excited at the thought that it might be from Ida, until I saw the sender's name.

It was as though a huge fist had struck me in the gut and winded me.

I thought I'd deleted this number from my phone years ago and blocked it, just to make doubly sure.

The teenager next to me turned the volume up even further.

*I'm sorry, bro, if you can't handle your ho.*

Under normal circumstances, the misogyny in these lyrics would have annoyed me, but now it didn't stir me at all. I stared at my phoned, numbed.

I'd made the mistake of thinking I'd put her behind me once and for all.

Just one message, and she was back in my life as though she'd never gone. But why on earth did she want to contact me now?

I stared out of the bus window as though the man pushing a buggy or the old woman crossing the road might have given me an answer. Their lives carried on just as before, while mine was hanging from a suspension bridge that had just collapsed.

What did she want from me?

I mulled the question in my mind. I was convinced that this text message contained a request—no, knowing who had sent it—a command. She wanted me to dance to her tune.

It was hard to sit still. I fidgeted in my seat, tried to calm myself down by counting the number of streetlamps along the pavement. Even for a problem like this, there must be a solution.

But there wasn't.

There was nothing I could do. She was in control. Just like before.

What if I just didn't read the message? What if I were to delete it and block the number again, pretend I'd never even received it?

She must have thought of all this when she sent the message. What if I didn't read it? But she knew the same as I did. One text message, and I was back under her control. I couldn't not open the message. I was like a Pavlovian dog, I heard the sound of the text message and immediately started drooling. I hated myself, but I couldn't help myself.

I was about to open the message when a surprising thought popped into my head. Maybe this was all a misunderstanding. I almost laughed out loud. She must have intended this message for someone else, some other Arto. Or an Aaro or an Arvi. Maybe my name was the last 'A' in her contacts list, and after me there was a Beata or a Benny. Her finger must have slipped onto the wrong name at the crucial moment, just as she was about to send the message to Auli or Aura. One wrong move and my whole life almost careered off course.

I felt lighter, as though I'd just dodged a bullet, as though someone had yanked me to safety at the last moment.

I wiped the corner of my eye and mentally thanked my lucky stars. I had Ida, my beautiful daughter, I had a job, I was healthy—yes, I'd managed to get my drinking under control—and Ida was healthy too. What else could I wish for?

I was about to put my phone back in my bag when another thought occurred to me. What did the message actually say? It wasn't intended for my eyes, but if I were to open it, I wouldn't be breaking any confidentiality rules. By law, it's a criminal offence to read another person's text messages. But the message had been sent to me. If I hadn't stopped to think about it, I would have opened the message as soon as it had arrived before realizing it wasn't actually meant for me.

The corners of my mouth crept into a smile, and a sense of *Schadenfreude* bubbled in my chest like champagne. A grown woman who didn't know how to use her phone but sent messages to all and sundry! She'd probably noticed her mistake and was already squirming with embarrassment.

I was about to open the message, but I wanted to draw out the feeling of delight at her misfortune. I decided to open the message only once I got home, perhaps enjoy an aromatic whisky on the side.

What kind of national secrets was she about to reveal against her will? I was intrigued. Was she opening her heart to a friend?

The bus stopped at the terminus, and I got off. It was as though I'd stepped out onto a bed of candyfloss. I felt no guilt at my nasty thoughts because I remembered how she had enjoyed humiliating me in the past.

Once I got home, I couldn't wait a moment longer but opened the message as soon as I closed the door behind me. Ida greeted me in the hallway, but I barely noticed her.

I had to lean against the wall.

The message was not meant for someone else.

It was meant for me.

Now everything was going to start from the beginning again.

The chorus of the song I'd heard in the boy's headphones started ringing in my head.

*Kill the bitch!*

# Ida

Once back home, I noticed that my dad had opened the curtains in my room. I quickly pulled them shut again. He had a habit of joking that I avoided daylight like Count Orlok. But his nervous chuckle revealed that, to him, it wasn't really a joke.

I switched on my laptop and opened up a browser. The picture of me that the guy with the hairy legs had taken on the square had already appeared on the websites of all the tabloids. Someone had drawn a red circle around my raised middle finger, as if the reader would otherwise be unable to see what kind of gesture I was giving.

I clenched the mouse in my hand. Showing that guy the middle finger didn't feel like such a good idea any more. As if it had ever been a good idea. The piece was entitled *Does Ida the Psycho Shrink Survivor Need Another Shrink?* Scorn and derision disguised as righteous concern. That the question itself was warranted. And the answer was obvious.

My dad would have been proud of me if he'd known I'd decided not to read the comments section. He thought it didn't matter what people said about me in the print media or on social media. I knew the truth, and that was all that mattered. But I didn't accept that everybody felt they had the right to twist my life into the version they wanted to hear. I wanted to take control of my own life. Because that wasn't possible, I at least wanted to follow what other people wrote about me.

I heard the front door. My dad hung his bag in the hallway but didn't look up from his phone; he didn't even respond to my hello, though I went to meet him. He looked like he was in a world of his own. Once he'd read the text message, he finally turned his attention to me.

He mumbled that he still had a few work things to take care of, then went to his office and locked the door behind him.

You would have thought that alcoholism might have made him better at coming up with more credible excuses, but apparently not.

I focused my thoughts on the body in Hakaniemi. Somehow, I imagined I'd be able to solve the mystery by myself. But what mystery? The death had already been deemed an accident. There was no mystery to solve.

I returned to my laptop and started making notes about the Hakaniemi case.

I decided to go into the kitchen to fetch a glass of water. When I stood up, I noticed there was a blood-red streak on my trouser leg, right across the thigh. It must have got there while I was lying in the chalk outline.

I turned on the tap and let the water run, then heard a phone ringing. The walls in our apartment were so badly soundproofed that I wasn't sure whether it was my dad's phone or whether it belonged to one of the neighbours. In any case, someone eventually picked up. I could make out the odd word here and there.

'No!'

The speaker seemed startled at his own shout. He lowered his voice, and then I couldn't hear what he was saying. All I could make out were his footsteps. He was pacing nervously back and forth, seemingly trying to clear his thoughts.

A moment later, the volume rose again.

'That was then, this is now!'

Silence.

'What happened between us was a mistake.'

What a cliché! I almost felt like laughing. As if the speaker was a character in a Mills & Boon novel! Maybe the voice was coming from the television. Maybe the neighbours were watching a corny soap opera with the volume turned up.

Bang!

Someone punched a fist into the wall.

I flinched. It must have been my dad. He often lost his temper when the neighbours were talking too loudly.

The punch had the desired effect. The speaker fell silent.

# Kerttu

The scissors clattered as they fell to the floor. I had been reliving my most important teenage memory, but now I was back in my office, sitting at my desk.

I picked up the scissors and continued cutting out the angel from my collection of pictures, as if nothing had happened. It annoyed me that I found it so hard to concentrate on the task I had given myself. I walked to the bulletin board at the back of the room, stopped in front of it for a moment and wondered where to attach the picture of the angel. I decided it would be nicest in the top right-hand corner of the board with a fire-alarm-red pin.

Apart from the angel, the bulletin board was still empty, but during the course of the investigation I would fill it with notes, newspaper clippings, anything that might be associated with the murder or—the thought was so horrifying that I could barely bring myself to think it—murders.

Each time a case ended, I was able to gather up the Post-it notes, the receipts, the scribbled notes, everything that had accumulated on the board through the course of an investigation, and file it away in boxes in the archive where evidence was stored, and then I was able to look at the board afresh, now blank again after such a long time. At these moments, a magnificent silence filled the room, one that always ended far too soon.

A set of knuckles rapped against the door. It was Koivuvyö. He didn't wait for my instruction to enter but marched into my office as if it were his own, though I had reprimanded him for this countless times.

The beach. The sand. The waves.

As always when he entered my office, Koivuvyö glanced first at the bulletin board, and when he noticed that something had appeared on it, he walked up to it, his brow furrowed.

'Tiilihella is asking whether you've got an action plan for the investigation.'

'Are you Tiilihella's messenger now? Can't you see I've got my hands full?'

Koivuvyö left the room. A moment later, I heard laughter in the corridor. He must have bumped into one of our colleagues and complained about my methods. Yes, I could make out what he was saying, clear as a bell.

'Leppänen's collecting stickers again.'

I felt like walking out into the corridor and giving Koivuvyö a piece of my mind. We were in a rut that I didn't know how to break out of. I wanted to start from scratch, but perhaps the only way of communicating with him was by arguing. *Tough love*, Tiilihella had called it, when I'd tried to explain the problems that Koivuvyö and I were having. I had left Tiilihella's office cursing to myself.

I tried to quell my anger. If it came to the crunch, Koivuvyö would have given his life for me. As would I for him.

I stared intensely at the board until I had a sudden idea. I had to tell Tiilihella about it immediately.

I stopped for a moment and ran my fingers across the grooves I'd cut into my office door with a knife. Nobody in the whole department had hunted down as many killers as I had.

The events in Dresden began pushing their way into my mind. Again, I pushed them back just as forcefully.

But I didn't want to forget Esko's face.

# Ida

Sugar Kane pouted her lips in preparation for that famous *boop-boop-a-doop*! My dad and I were rewatching *Some Like It Hot*. And he was trying to fatten me up again. The table was laden with kilocalories in the form of crisps, biscuits and sweets. I reached over and took a single crisp out of the bowl to keep him happy, and I caught a whiff of his breath. It smelt of garlic.

The beep of a text message took our attention from Marilyn. My dad pretended to carry on watching the film, but in fact he was trying to peer over my shoulder to see who the message was from. I managed to hide the screen from him, but there was no escaping his nosy questions.

'Your secret admirer again?'

He nudged me with his elbow and started humming out of tune. I didn't recognize the song, but I had a suspicion it might have been 'Love Me Tender'.

I started scratching at my cuticles again. My dad handed me a tissue to wipe the blood from my fingers. I felt like shouting in his face: See me! But I settled for clenching my hand into a fist instead and imagined the fist striking my dad in the face, again and again. First the nose, then both cheeks.

I'd explained myself to him till I was blue in the face, but he still didn't understand. He sat there smiling, and his smile only made me angrier. Why couldn't he ever see me the way

I was—sick, broken and unworthy? Why couldn't he just let me recover from my traumas? Why couldn't he give me time?

I would forever have to drag my past behind me like a train made of thick, night-dark velvet.

I decided to read the message only once I'd returned to my room, once we'd finished watching the film.

Perhaps that might have been the time to come clean and tell him the truth, but I couldn't bring myself to do it.

His heart had been fluttering ever since I'd got the second message from the same sender in the office canteen.

I'd been caught out by my own lies, though I hadn't actually lied to him. My dad had misinterpreted my roundabout answer. 'It's just someone I met,' I'd said. He imagined I had some kind of romance on the go. And by now it was too hard to correct that misunderstanding. Why couldn't he just understand that I didn't have it in me to be in a relationship?

The film finally came to an end, and we said goodnight.

I couldn't bring myself to open the message right away. I didn't want to know what it said. I didn't want to know anything about it.

I hadn't responded to either of the two previous messages. I wasn't sure whether I'd understood what they meant. I didn't even know whether whoever had sent them really wanted me to understand them or not. Or was the point just to tease me, like a cat playing with a shrew. I couldn't answer until I was sure what the sender meant. I didn't want to make any unfounded allegations.

But eventually I opened the message.

It must have been a sick joke.

# Kerttu

'Tell me.'

If there was anything at the Pasila police station that was used even more sparingly than money, it was words.

I took a cushion from the chair, sat down and held the cushion against my chest, like a buffer to protect me from Tiilihella. The cushion was embroidered with a police horse, its muzzle too large in proportion to its body.

Tiilihella looked at me expectantly.

'As you know, we still don't have any physical evidence besides the serial killer's diary. What if we published extracts from it in the media?'

'Why on earth would we do that?'

'Someone might recognize the handwriting.'

Tiilihella stood up and walked beside me, as though he was afraid that at any moment I might escape and run straight to the offices of *Helsinki Today*.

'Under no circumstances! A media circus and mass hysteria are the last things we need! Nobody knows there's a serial killer on the loose, and it's going to stay that way until we've got him in custody.'

'The investigation has reached an impasse. We have to try something, before the killer strikes again!'

My words had risen to a shout. I pulled thin threads from the police horse's tail, and they fell into my lap and got stuck to my trousers.

'Patience, Leppänen! I won't ruin another case by leaking information to the press too early in the investigation.'

I avoided Tiilihella's eyes and hoped he wouldn't notice I was blushing. The previous spring we had made the mistake of publishing the identifying characteristics of a man suspected of killing a famous singer, though the eyewitness's description had been very vague indeed. Because the singer was so popular, the whole country ended up talking about the case, and every man and his dog had wanted to play a part in solving the crime.

The phones at the station rang off the hook as helpful citizens began inundating us with unfounded claims. There were deranged conspiracy theorists, mediums who claimed to have made contact with the singer from beyond the grave—everyone was involved in the crime, from the president to Charlie Chaplin—and then there were the real tinfoil hats who believed the singer wasn't dead at all but had turned into an alien and was now living safely on Titan, Saturn's largest moon.

We had wasted resources looking into baseless tips when we could have been focusing on the investigation itself. The case could have gone cold if the culprit hadn't come to regret what he had done, confessed and handed himself in to the police.

I slipped away to my office and kicked the filing cabinet. It didn't help; my anger didn't abate, and now I'd stubbed my toe. It would be a long time before I would be able to clear the bulletin board again.

I opened the safe. Why had a grown man decided to keep a diary that was more suited to a little girl and not a black-covered notebook or a blue school jotter?

A light bulb came on in my mind.

What if the killer wasn't a man after all?

Not a little girl, obviously, but a woman, a young woman?

I had assumed unquestioningly that the sex of the serial killer was obvious. Someone might ask why I was so prejudiced towards men—and women too, in fact, as if their biology made them too sensitive to commit such heinous crimes.

My teacher Heiskanen would have disliked this logical leap. To him, statistics were like a religion. Each time he gave us students a new case to solve, he was able to recite the facts and statistics related to the case from memory: how many homicides had been carried out in Finland using a pruning hook; how many crimes had been committed in Hakunila in the last five years; the probability that the victim and the perpetrator knew each other before the homicide took place.

'There's nothing glamorous about police work! Eighty per cent of people who commit a homicide are drunk at the time, and even those are mostly manslaughters that the drunks commit in a fit of rage,' Heiskanen used to say at the end of every lecture to anyone who was still awake.

Even at the time, I was convinced that a blind faith in statistics could cause us to overlook anomalies. But Heiskanen's teaching still lingered at the back of my mind.

Only around fifteen per cent of serial killers are female. Or, as Heiskanen would have presented the same statistic, up to eighty-five per cent of serial killers are male.

Statistically speaking, therefore, it was unlikely that the serial killer who had been keeping this diary was a woman. Far too unlikely, Heiskanen would have concluded.

Unlikely, but not impossible, I concluded.

I called Koivuvyö and tasked him with digging up all the information he could find about any female inmates who had been serving time for murder or attempted murder and who had been released from prison within the last ten years.

After thinking this through a moment longer, I called him again.

I asked him to find all available information about women released from psychiatric hospitals and who had been sectioned for the same reasons within the same timeframe.

I felt like the knot was finally tightening around my killer.

# Ida

I grabbed my victim's limp, dangling hand, pressed the tip of my finger tightly against her wrist and felt her weak pulse.

In my other hand, I squeezed my dad's old Swiss army knife. This knife had never let me down. In the past I'd cut my own skin with it, and now my wrists were covered in scars that looked like train tracks. I'd never wielded the knife against anyone except myself. I'd certainly never used it for real, freeing the spirit from the body.

I carefully placed the blade against the victim's wrist, then made three thin cuts, pale and hesitant as a virgin bride on her wedding night. My victim didn't put up a fight; she had fallen asleep in the bathtub hours before I arrived.

Perhaps through the soupy fog of drunkenness, she might have thought this was some kind of apparition. Perhaps in her eyes I was an angel or a devil. To me, she was a sacrificial lamb. I let her bleed out in the bathtub like a cow in the slaughterhouse.

My victim could expect either the lascivious flames of eternal hellfire licking around her or the blinding lights of heaven, depending on her faith. But, given the kind of life she had lived, I guessed she didn't believe in anything and hadn't for a very long time. Her life hadn't given her any reason for faith. Every time she'd desperately tried to grab hold of something worth living for, someone had stamped on her fingers.

Half an hour had passed since I'd politely rung my victim's doorbell, in case she was still conscious.

The apartment was situated in Sörnäinen, a rough area infamous for drink and drugs, on the ground floor of a block built in the 1920s. I'd walked past this house countless times and peered in through the window as the woman's life slowly spiralled out of control.

My victim was a full-time drunk. Her mornings always began in exactly the same way. She started drinking at ten and worked hard at it all day, like a frenzied workaholic civil servant who wasn't content until every form had been copied three times and her stamp had run out of ink. She had started the day watching TV on the leather sofa in the living room. By evening, she had already passed out. Today she had decided to take a bath but hadn't even managed to turn on the tap before losing consciousness.

To be honest, it was like winning the lottery that my victim had passed out in the tub without a shred of clothing on: it meant I didn't have to undress her or carry her. It was as if she'd read my thoughts, worked out what I was planning and done everything she could to make it easy for me. It was obvious she wanted to die. But she didn't have it in her to take her own life. So, she'd left the dirty work to me.

I tightened my grip on her wrist, pressed the knife deeper into the flesh. Amid the faint cuts, there appeared a wider slash. Blood started to gush from the wound like water from a babbling mountain spring.

My hands did not waver. I was like an architect drawing a town plan or an artist painting tiny details on a canvas, like curls of fair hair on his muse's forehead.

The victim's wrist quivered, but not even the pain could

rouse her from her slumber. I'd been steeling myself to smash her head against the edge of the bathtub if she suddenly came to.

I propped her bleeding wrist on the edge of the tub and turned on the tap. I had no idea what made people slit their wrists in a bath full of running water. Was there a good reason for this? And if so, what was it? I'd seen plenty of films where people committed suicide following this exact ritual. I imagined my victim must have seen these films too. The more cinematic her suicide, the more authentic it would look. At least, that's what I hoped. Of course, the police would know why you had to run the tap while bleeding to death—or had the movies got it all wrong? If so, surely the police wouldn't expect my victim to have known that.

I was ready.

I didn't know when I'd next get an invitation to carry out my duties.

# Kerttu

I looked over Koivuvyö's list. At my request, he had gathered information on any women who had recently been convicted of murder or attempted murder. Koivuvyö, Nikulainen and, to my surprise, an impatient-looking Tiilihella filed into the conference room one after the other. Tiilihella didn't usually attend our meetings. Having said that, we weren't usually hunting a serial killer.

Tiilihella looked at the time.

'So, what's new?'

When Tiilihella had forbidden me from contacting the media, I'd had no option but to take a more drastic, desperate route. I explained that I had sent a copy of a few pages from the diary to a graphologist in case the same handwriting had come up in previous cases. This was extremely unlikely, as our serial killer was careful and meticulous and wouldn't have offered us the diary on a silver platter if the handwriting was already in the system.

Tiilihella seemed to agree with me that this was futile, as he simply scoffed, clearly waiting for me to say something more constructive.

I switched on the projector and put the slide in place. Tiilihella muttered something under his breath. He was worried I might have a dozen slides to get through, though I simply wanted to show everybody Koivuvyö's list.

Nonetheless, Koivuvyö had handed out copies of the list to everyone in the room.

'What's all this about?' asked Tiilihella.

I explained that I suspected the killer might be a woman. Or rather, that the killer wasn't necessarily a man.

Again, I could hear Heiskanen's voice in the back of my mind.

*For decades and to the present day, the most common form of homicide in Finland is when a man kills his drinking buddy with a kitchen knife in a private residence.*

I was certain that Tiilihella considered the matter in much the same way as Heiskanen.

'Well, that's certainly a unique angle on the case,' he scoffed again.

I gritted my teeth. I felt like asking him what was so funny about the idea, but I didn't; he hadn't rejected it out of hand.

'Very well, let's assume for a moment that the killer is female,' he went on grudgingly. 'Koivuvyö and Nikulainen, start going through this list. Find out where these women were at the time of the axe murder and establish whether they have an alibi. But let's not forget the possibility that the culprit might be a man after all.'

Tiilihella began scrutinizing the list, and we followed his example. I was familiar with most of these names; I had led investigations into their crimes too.

Tiilihella produced a small evidence bag from his jacket pocket and took out a calligraphy pen that had leaked cobalt-blue ink into the bag. Next to one of the names, he made the neatest cross I'd ever seen.

Tiilihella handed his list to Koivuvyö.

'Start with her. Find out whether any of the others used an axe to kill their victims.'

Koivuvyö nodded and pointed to another name on the list.

'I was involved in this investigation.'

Koivuvyö was always so modest. He hadn't just investigated the case; he had solved it. Most Finns had read about the case in the headlines, and it had kept the Turku police busy for a long time. A woman had killed her employer and managed to frame a former colleague for the murder. She had recently been made redundant and was bitter about being let go. Koivuvyö had managed to break the killer during interrogation, and she had confessed to the crime.

The phone rang in the conference room. Tiilihella answered. A moment later, he hung up and said simply:

'We've got a body.'

# Ida

My dad was feverishly bashing his computer keyboard. Nobody in the office was left in any doubt as to what he thought about writing an obituary for a long-forgotten author. He would much rather have been putting together an in-depth report on the cartel running housing associations around the city or on the underground economy in the building trade.

Two reporters walked past my desk, chatting to each other. One of them was explaining that there had been massive water damage in the apartment block where he lived in Sörnäinen, as one of the tenants had committed suicide by slashing her wrists in the bathtub. Before her death, she'd turned on the tap and left it running. The other residents only noticed something was amiss when water started flowing into the corridor.

I could almost see the woman lying naked in the bathtub, her eyes wide open. Her gaze tormented me. I could feel my T-shirt sticking to my back with sweat.

I glanced around, as though I'd been caught in the act. I stood up and pretended to stretch though, in fact, I was trying to listen in on their conversation, to see if they said anything else about the deceased. I sat down again, started rapping my knuckles against the desk, though I knew I was disturbing my dad's concentration.

I couldn't sit still and stood up again. I muttered something to my dad, told him I was going for a cigarette. I tried to slow my steps so as not to burst into a run as I headed out to the balcony.

There was nobody else there, and Visalahti was nowhere to be seen. I took a lighter and a packet of cigarettes from my jeans pocket and tried to light a cigarette. I had to struggle against gusts of wind, but eventually managed to light up and quickly took a few deep drags. It didn't calm me down. My hands were still trembling, and my heart was pounding frantically.

I heard the wail of a police car in the street and tried to push my vertigo to one side for a moment. I stepped closer to the railing, carefully peered over the edge. The police car pulled up right outside the front door of *Helsinki Today*, its brakes screeching.

The sound felt like a warning to me. The police had realized their mistake, and now they were here to get me. This was my last chance to make a run for it.

I rushed back inside and stopped in the middle of the office, at a loss. I hurried to my desk and snatched my bag from the back of my seat. I tried to muster as normal a tone of voice as I could as I told my dad that I had such stomach ache that I had to go home for the rest of the day.

And just as I'd feared, my dad started making a fuss. He was trying to sound as calm as possible, though his twitching leg showed his worry at my sudden illness. Would I be able to get home by myself? Did I need anything from the shop?

There was only one way to shut him up. I didn't want to resort to this; it was embarrassing all round.

'It's period pain.'

He stammered, flummoxed: 'Okay, see you this evening, when I get back from work.'

In the lift, I was worried that the police might be waiting for me in the lobby.

Once the lift finally reached the ground floor, I peered out through its door, and when I couldn't see any police in the lobby, I plucked up the courage to step out.

I slowly walked towards the exit, ready to turn on my heels and run back to the lift at any moment.

I was certain that everyone could see the beads of sweat on my forehead. I blinked and shook my arms in an attempt to release some tension. That didn't help either.

By the time I finally made it outside the building, the police car was gone.

# Kerttu

The naked old woman in the bathtub stared at me as though she was pleading for help. I assumed that the only witness to her final moments was the lost-looking plastic duck floating in the bathwater.

This was a routine case, a suicide. That's what the first responders had concluded, but I was so frustrated at the lack of progress in the serial-killer case that I had decided to examine every body found in the city personally until we apprehended the killer.

When I'd arrived at the apartment, the forensic officers were just leaving.

I walked into the bathroom. Inside, it was like a Jackson Pollock painting. The tiles were covered in blood spatter, as though the last thing the woman lying in the bath had tried to do was climb out of her enamel coffin but had only succeeded in messing up the floor and the walls.

I picked up a red-handled Swiss army knife from the floor and bagged it as evidence. The blade looked blunt. The deceased would have needed to use a lot of force to slit her wrists with this.

The doorbell rang. I had been lecturing at the police academy for years now, and I always invited the students to join me and examine a crime scene in this initial phase, even though it was technically illegal.

Tiilihella knew I didn't always do things by the book. Nonetheless, he thought it was immaterial how I took care of my work, as long as I caught the culprits. I hated authority figures, and I don't think I would have been able to work under someone who was a real stickler for the rules. There was a certain irony that someone like me, who was constantly pushing back against the system, had ended up in the police force.

For a long time now, I had been keen to show the first-year students how easy it was to distinguish a suicide committed with a knife or other sharp object from a murder, and that was why I had asked Koivuvyö to get them down to the scene.

'Right, kids, follow me.'

I led the students into the bathroom. They lined up around the bath. Some of them tried to get through the situation by staring at the tiles, while others blinked, as though they could only take in what they saw in small doses. Thankfully there was a toilet in the bathroom, in case any of them felt queasy.

I gripped the body's right wrist. One of the students—a woman who looked much younger than her years—flinched so violently that she accidentally shoved me with her elbow. My nitrile glove was too small; it squeaked annoyingly as I tried to examine the wrist. One of the students sniggered, then quickly turned away, thinking I might not notice his reaction. I couldn't even bring myself to be angry at him, but I could feel my pulse increasing. The students were essentially children, as this immature behaviour demonstrated.

There was one deep cut in the deceased's wrist and three shallower cuts around it. This was a standard pattern. People who slit their wrists often left smaller cuts alongside the main wound. I explained to the students that the woman had died from loss of blood caused by the fatal cut. I showed the students the cuts and gave them a task.

I wanted them to consider the reason for these different cuts on the woman's wrist.

The students had now seen their first official suicide case; I hoped they had never had to experience such violent, self-destructive death before their studies.

I asked the students to go to a café downtown to discuss the matter. I promised to join them once I had checked something that had been bothering me.

The woman's apartment was in a terrible state. As I'd stepped inside, I had instinctively covered my nose and mouth with my hand before putting on a surgical mask. I handed them out to the students when they arrived too. But even the masks couldn't filter out the repulsive smell of tobacco, old fish, rotten eggs and goodness knows what else.

The stench was laced with the scent of a musky perfume. I guessed it was Yves Saint Laurent's Opium, a particularly spicy fragrance.

In the kitchen, the stink of rotten food grew even stronger. The sink was full of dirty dishes covered in dried food. The fridge door had been left open. Inside there was nothing but an opened box of liver casserole and a tube of mustard, squeezed almost empty.

From the cutlery drawer, I gathered all the knives and laid them out in a neat row on the dining table, before holding them up one by one to examine the blades.

As expected, the dinner knives were blunt, but I had found two other knives in the drawer—a bread knife with a brown wooden handle and a long knife with a black plastic handle—both of which were sharper than the Swiss army knife that the woman had used.

Why would someone contemplating suicide use a blunt Swiss army knife instead of one of these much sharper ones?

I decided to take them with me too.

I walked across the Long Bridge and headed back to the city centre. The sun warmed my face, as if to taunt the deceased woman's family by shining on the day when they faced perhaps the greatest tragedy of their lives.

I spotted the group of students at the back of the café. I ordered a cup of tea and a doughnut, though I can't eat doughnuts without making a mess. The students gladly made space for me at their table. I sat down among them like Jesus at the Last Supper.

Colour had gradually returned to the students' cheeks, though none of them had dared order food just yet. The deceased's face, smeared with blood, was still foremost in their minds.

I had already come to accept the students' choice of career. Each time I met a new intake, I felt like telling them it wasn't too late to back out: there was still time to give up or change career. But because I wanted to teach them, I had to keep my mouth shut. And yet it made me sad to see them at lectures and to know everything they were about to lose because of their career choice.

Things I too had lost.

After taking a comforting sip from my cup, I asked the students to tell me how they had answered the question I'd posed them. Was there a born homicide investigator among them? Someone not just with good grades but with intuition too—and the bravery to use it.

'Come on, kids, tell me what you've got!'

The students presented a variety of explanations they had come up with. It was a nervous-looking young woman who came up with the most daring theory. She almost whispered as she spoke. She suggested that the cuts on the deceased's wrist were some kind of sign and that the woman had been trying to tell us something.

But tell us *what*?

The student didn't know that.

Still, I respected the fact that she'd had the guts to present her theory. A police investigation proceeds best of all when the investigators can share ideas with one another, even those that seem far-fetched. I had tried to make our workplace an environment so non-judgemental that investigators felt they could come forward with any suggestions, no matter how outlandish.

Once they had all presented their theories, to my disappointment I had to conclude that none of them was right, though some of the youngsters had seemed very confident in their conclusions.

The deceased had not attempted suicide in the past using the same method, therefore the shallow cuts had not been made earlier than the deeper, fatal cut. We could tell this because all of the cuts were still oozing blood. She had not made the shallow cuts to mark spots that she planned to come back to later and make another, much deeper cut. She had not switched the Swiss army knife for a sharper knife halfway through in order to make deeper cuts.

In fact, as I explained to them, such shallow cuts are often found on the wrists of suicide victims. They are known as hesitation wounds.

The deceased wasn't sure whether to go through with the suicide or if she could stand the pain. So she tested herself, not the knife, by making three small cuts on the wrist first. Only once she was sure that she really wanted to go through with it did she make the fourth cut, right in the middle of the wrist.

Murderers, meanwhile, did not hesitate. If they tried to stage a murder as a suicide, they failed by cutting straight through the radial artery, because they didn't know that people with suicidal ideation often hesitated. Unless they too had attempted suicide, that is.

The students seemed relieved. Some of them had been convinced that the woman had in fact been murdered. Suicide seemed a less cruel way to die.

The nervous young woman took a thick notepad from her bag and began feverishly drawing something. I peered over her shoulder to get a better look. Her felt-tip pen danced across the paper, sketching a series of lines.

She was drawing the woman's wrist.

She indicated the positions of the different cuts in precisely the right places.

# Ida

A criminal always returns to the scene of the crime. But what about the victim? I could hardly believe I was walking along the winding path leading to the Bastard's cottage, the same place where he had imprisoned me both times he'd kidnapped me.

I hadn't told my dad about my plans. I could almost hear him warning me, telling me I shouldn't go out of my way to open up old wounds. He wouldn't have let me go to the cottage, not by myself at any rate. He would have insisted on coming with me, against my will, if necessary.

In fact, visiting the cottage might have been therapeutic for my dad. Unlike the first two times I'd been here, now he would have the chance to protect me. Still, I was more worried that he might have some kind of breakdown and I'd end up having to take care of him.

It was four years since I'd last been along this path. Back then, I'd been hidden under a tarpaulin in the back seat of the Bastard's car. I was sure of our destination, though through the tiny hole in the tarpaulin I couldn't really see where we were going. I knew there was a cage waiting for me, and at the bottom of that cage was the rug with that same bloodstain on it.

My blood.

When the Bastard had lifted me out of his car, I noticed that the cottage roof was covered in moss and some of the tiles had come loose. The garden was a tangle of grass and weeds with lupins and willowherb growing here and there. Mugwort rustled against the Bastard's bare shins as he waded through the knee-high jungle in shorts. He didn't notice the nettles growing among the other weeds until they stung his legs. After that, he bounded across the rest of the garden, swearing as he went.

I remember thinking that it looked like nobody had visited this cottage for years. Perhaps not since the first time the Bastard had kidnapped me, when I was ten years old.

Now the grass had been trampled underfoot. Instead of bluebells and timothy, the garden was strewn with empty cigarette packets and crushed cans of lager. I counted the black patches of singed grass, evidence of illegal bonfires. Four.

I tried to avoid the shards of broken beer bottles and accidentally stepped on a disposable barbecue. Half of a cheap sausage, blackened and charred, had been discarded on the tinfoil. It looked like it had been left there only recently.

Ants were already devouring this catch. Soon there would be nothing left of the sausage. If the ants worked at the same rate all day long, they would be able to carry it to their nest in a few days, one tiny piece at a time. I watched them at work. Their route took them to the roots of a pine tree.

The tree served as a guestbook.

*Leevi woz here.*
*Elias woz here 2.*
*I'm here!*

And so on. Almost all the visitors were men, but there were a few women too.

Someone had carved a skull into the tree's bark and written a name inside it. I had to peer at it for a while before I could read what it said.



A page torn from a porn magazine was nailed to the trunk. The elements hadn't yet pulled it free, so this might have been the sausage-scoffer's calling card. In the image, a woman with extraordinary breast implants grimaced with pain as a man dressed like a butcher screwed her.

I almost missed one of the inscriptions. It was carved so high up that I hadn't noticed it at first.



At one of their kill spots, members of the Manson family had daubed this misspelling of the name of the Beatles' famous hit on the fridge door in their victims' blood. The killer must have been dyslexic.

The front wall of the cottage was covered in a giant cross. I walked closer.

The cross was painted in blood.

Or some other liquid that uncannily resembled blood.

I went up the steps to the front door. On the first step, a snake was warming itself in the sunshine. I quickly stepped over it then crouched down to get a closer look. It turned out to be a used condom.

Did what the Bastard did to me really turn some people on so much that they felt the urge to have sex at the scene of the crime?

I gripped the door handle.

The door wouldn't open.

It wasn't locked. I was.

I couldn't cross the threshold and step inside the cottage.

I'd managed to escape this cottage twice before. I didn't want to find out whether the third time really was a charm. The Bastard would never get his hands on me again. Yet, when I thought about him, he was omnipotent. As if he had a crystal ball through which he could watch my every move and ambush me at the cottage.

The sausage-scoffer had left me one last clue: there was a small figure sketched on the front door in charcoal, no doubt from the barbecue. And written above the stick man—or, in this case, stick woman—were the words:

*I am Ida.*

The likeness between me and the drawing was obvious. More than that, it was like a photograph of me taken four years ago. Back then my head looked disproportionately large compared to my scrawny, insect-like arms and legs. Now there was a little more flesh on my bones.

I pulled down the sleeve of my hoodie to cover my hand and started wiping the drawing away.

My hand stopped mid-motion.

I'd seen this figure before.

I shook my head. I imagined fear and anxiety shrinking

into tiny droplets flying here and there as if from a dog shaking itself dry.

The bench at the edge of Hakaniemi Square.

The same image had been carved into the bench with a knife. It was so small that I could barely make it out.

*I am Ida.*

The glint of sunlight caught a rhombus-shaped shard of glass on the steps. The flash blinded me. I picked up the shard, cut a slit in my thumb.

For a moment, there was nothing else in the world but pain.

Then I found myself standing on the steps outside the cottage once more, and my chest seemed to tighten.

I took a tissue from my pocket and wrapped it around my thumb. The bleeding stopped almost immediately. It wasn't a deep cut.

What might it look like inside the cottage? The lock had been broken ages ago. My admirers must have made off with everything that had once been in the cottage.

The kitchen table had been knocked over. The wooden chairs had been hurled against the walls, and they had fallen to pieces. Dishes lay smashed on the floor. The shelves had been removed from all the old cupboards. The rug that used to cover the hatch leading down to the basement had been torn to shreds.

Suddenly, an image of the cage appeared in my mind.

I had to get out of here.

I started running as fast as I could. I heard thuds as my feet thumped against the path. I carried on running until I reached the main road and saw the bus stop. I sat down on the bench, panting, held my head between my knees, tried to steady my breathing. I wiped my wet cheeks, pressed a fingernail into the cut on my thumb.

What had I been expecting? I should have known! And I did know.

The only way to get away from this cottage was to run for your life.

# Kerttu

I rubbed my sweaty palms against my thighs before plucking up the courage to ring the doorbell.

Nobody came to open. I rang a second time. I was already enjoying the sense of relief and had almost turned around when the door opened with a squeal, as if someone had accidentally stood on a dog's tail.

I looked up and saw the disappointed face of Eetu Metsäkankare.

Eetu looked as though he had been holding on to a faint hope all this time, hope that someone had come to visit him who might change the course of his life; perhaps even a singing telegram telling him he had won the lottery or someone from the job centre who wanted to tell him in person that he had just secured the first job in his life.

Eetu turned and lazily shuffled into the living room. He was limping on his left leg. From the hallway, a trail of muddy footprints led further into the apartment. If this apartment were a crime scene, I would have whooped with joy. I knocked the worst bits of mud from my shoes onto the doormat. The yard outside was so full of potholes and puddles that it had been pointless trying to avoid them. I followed him without bothering to take off my shoes.

With some difficulty, Eetu sat down in an armchair, winced with pain, lit a new cigarette from the ember of his previous one and gestured me towards the same dirty brown sofa that I sat on once a year for a few hours each time.

I picked up yesterday's *Helsinki Today* from the table, carefully placed it on the sofa and sat on the paper. Eetu scoffed at the familiar procedure. He took a drag on his cigarette, looked me up and down, feigning indifference, and waited for me to tell him some news.

I don't know whether he really believed that one day he would find out who had murdered his little brother Janne all those decades ago.

If he did believe it, he was the only one.

And just as Eetu has asked me his question in perfect silence, I responded without opening my mouth and simply shrugged my shoulders.

His expression didn't so much as flinch. Was it so important to him to maintain the hard-guy image, though I of all people knew it was nothing but a façade? Or had he finally given up hope that I would ever find Janne's killer? Was this routine of ours that repeated unaltered year upon year nothing but a formality to him, something that had become so important to him that now he couldn't give it up?

But Eetu wasn't the only one hiding his true feelings.

I pretended that the fact I still hadn't caught Janne's killer hadn't torn my soul to shreds.

Janne's photograph was still in the same place on the sun-bleached Lundia bookcase where Eetu didn't keep any books, only miscellaneous junk. To the left of the photograph was a certificate for coming third in the pool championships at the Watering Hole five years ago, and to the right was the collar of Eetu's best friend, his dog Rekku who had died a few years before. In the framed photograph, a young Janne was smiling, showing off his first ever school certificate.

Eetu stood up, walked to the window and scratched his head. A group of drunks had taken over the small woodland at the back of the plot and was making an almighty racket. Eetu was the only one of them who still hadn't drunk away his apartment, but this was only a matter of time.

I was startled. For a moment, he looked just like Janne, or rather, he looked like what I imagined Janne might have looked like, wrinkles and all, had he still been alive.

The impression only lasted a moment, then Eetu turned his head.

Nonetheless, a paralysing sense of guilt had already consumed me.

He opened the window and shouted to his mates, telling them he would join them soon. He didn't want his drinking buddies to come round while there was a pig on the couch.

Koivuvyö was the only one who knew that I still visited Eetu. It was pointless trying to hide anything from him; I didn't know anyone who was as good an interrogator as him. I'd told him about Eetu a few months ago at the end of an evening in the pub. We'd been at the Watering Hole to celebrate my birthday when, just before last orders, the confession had slipped out of my mouth.

Koivuvyö had shaken his head.

'Why do you torture yourself like this? It doesn't make you a better person.'

The fact that he didn't understand me hurt more than I liked to admit.

'If I can shake off the guilt, what will I have left?'

A look of pity flickered across Koivuvyö's face, though he quickly managed to suppress it. He knew I didn't need anybody's pity, least of all his.

I knew how this was going to play out.

I gripped my glass and took a quick gulp of vodka. I could feel the burning sensation as the liquor set my throat on fire.

'Is it safe for you to visit Eetu alone?'

Police officers always work in pairs, and for good reason. Attending a scene alone was out of the question. Eetu had initially been suspected of Janne's murder, because the brothers were on bad terms. What's more, they had had an argument on the day of Janne's death, and they had even got into a fight. Janne fancied Eetu's girlfriend, and during her interrogation the girlfriend had revealed that Eetu had decided to teach his brother a lesson.

Koivuvyö was right. I was putting my life at risk by visiting Eetu. (It will come as no surprise then that I had been keeping these meetings from Tiilihella.) But Koivuvyö knew that his words were falling on deaf ears. Police officers are stubborn by nature. It's a character trait that has taken many of us to an early grave.

My subordinate picked up his glass, sipped and changed the subject. At that moment, I realized that Koivuvyö had his own Jannes and didn't want to be reminded of them.

Eetu flicked ash into an empty pizza box that looked like it had been serving as an ashtray for some time now. He had nobody left, nobody who loved Janne as much as he did.

The first time Eetu had called me was when he'd found out about his parents' death. He insinuated that he had new information about Janne's murder, but I had only been sitting on his sofa for fifteen minutes before I realized that he simply wanted to talk about his brother with someone he knew was as affected by his death as he was.

Which of us was the worst masochist, me or Eetu? We were both torturing ourselves and each other by meeting up every year on the anniversary of Janne's death. Eetu never let me down. His anger was still as raw as it had been that morning when I brought the terrible news to his family. And because the culprit still hadn't been caught—because *I* had not caught the culprit; you see how I tried to hide behind the passive—his rage was aimed at me and me alone.

For me, Janne's murder had become a symbol of all my myriad failures.

Eetu walked into the kitchen and returned a moment later with two bottles of beer. I had come prepared with the exact change. I took my purse out of my handbag. Eetu didn't offer beer to the cops for free, especially not the cop who had screwed up his brother's murder investigation.

Over the years, he had become even more taciturn, as though he had finally understood that there was no magic word that could bring Janne back, not even if he had gone through his entire vocabulary with me.

We had nothing left to say to each other. We drank our beer in silence. When our bottles were empty, he fetched us two more and again I paid for my own. Then it was time for me to leave.

Eetu showed me to the door, not out of politeness but to make sure that I really left.

I looked behind the door leading into the hallway. Raphael's angels were hiding there. I had given Eetu this reproduction on the first anniversary of Janne's death. It felt a little maca-bre to give Eetu a gift on the anniversary of his brother's murder, but somehow, I felt this was the way I needed to honour Janne's memory. I had bought that picture, though I'd been certain Eetu would tear it up and certainly not put it up on his wall.

But he had opened the parcel as enthusiastically as I imagined him opening Christmas presents as a child. Perhaps nobody had given him Christmas presents when he was a child, and if they had, he probably hadn't got nearly as many as other children.

Once he had opened the parcel to reveal the rolled-up picture, Eetu rolled his eyes with the present in his hands before I took hold of it and helped him to unroll it so that he could see it.

'Proper art, eh?'

I'd never heard Eetu chuckle with laughter before, and I've never heard it since.

Now just as I stepped into the corridor, he called after me, 'When are you going to stop spying on me? When will you get it into your head I'm not guilty?'

I didn't need to restrain him; my expression was enough to tell him not to try anything with me. Obediently, he withdrew back into his apartment.

All these years, I had been holding back the anger I felt towards Eetu. Now that I had the opportunity to show him what I really thought of him, I felt relief.

His words echoed through my mind on the drive back to Pasila.

This was the best confession I would ever get out of him.

# Ida

I pressed a hand on the youngster's back and pushed him against the stone wall of the railway station. He slumped to the asphalt, lifeless. Only a few moments ago, he'd had no inkling that the grim reaper was waiting for him around the corner.

Something flashed inside me, something I'd never felt towards my victims before. I tried to latch on to the sensation. It kept slipping from my grasp like a piece of wet soap.

I crouched down next to him, held my hand in front of his mouth and confirmed what I already suspected: he was dead.

I'd completed the first stage of my task.

From my backpack, I took out all the props I needed for the next little bit of theatre: a scarf, a spoon, a bottle of water, a lighter, a syringe and a small baggie containing a generous dose of heroin. I'd bought the drugs only a few hours ago from a dealer who approached me at the train station.

I had no difficulty whatsoever in luring my victim with me. All I had to do was dangle the bag so he could see it. After that, he scurried after me like a rat after the Pied Piper.

I'd prepared myself for what was to come by watching *Christiane F.*—Uli Edel's gritty original version, of course. I tied the scarf around my victim's right arm, just above the elbow. Then I took the bottle and poured a few drops of water into the spoon, sprinkled the heroin into the water and prepared the dose by using the lighter to heat the spoon from beneath. Once it was ready, I pulled the drug up into the syringe.

Then I inserted the needle into the victim's vein. I was surprised at how easy it was to locate the vein. From looking at this junkie, you could tell he'd been injecting drugs for years. The gaunt, sunken cheeks, the dishevelled look and empty stare left no room for doubt. I'd expected his veins to be in much worse shape.

I'd spotted him by the main doors of the railway station where he was wandering around restlessly, trying to bum a cigarette or some spare change from the handful of nocturnal passers-by. It was already past midnight. Nobody disturbed me, and I was able to lure him away from prying eyes without the slightest trouble.

The police wouldn't suspect murder; they would put his death down to an overdose. It would be up to them to decide whether he had overdosed deliberately or by accident.

I packed my equipment back into my bag, left the victim's body lying next to the station and walked off towards the tram stop.

I'd only taken a few steps when I stopped in my tracks.

Something was wrong. Where was the jubilation, the exhilaration? That bubbling feeling, like being a bit tipsy, the feeling I'd experienced ever since the axe murder?

Suddenly a different sensation filled me, one that I hadn't been able to access before, despite my numerous attempts.

I felt sorry for my victim. The sensation consumed me. Even I couldn't fathom what I was doing. I walked back to him, sat down on the cold asphalt next to the body. I took his hand, squeezed it, as if that would make him rise from the dead.

All of a sudden, I couldn't bear to see his helpless face. What an idiot he'd been, to put his life in my hands.

I pulled my hand away, stood up.

I kicked the body in the stomach as hard as I could, then ran back to the tram stop. My mouth was sticky with pity, as if someone had stuffed it full of candyfloss.

I had no option but to return to the body.

# Kerttu

Tiilihella appeared in the corridor, said good morning and followed me into my office. It was only six thirty, and I'd thought I was the first to arrive at the station.

My boss was wearing an off-white woollen jumper, embroidered with the police logo: the lion with a sword. He saw that my eyes were drawn to the front of his sweater, and he looked embarrassed. He faithfully wore all his wife's creations, and Koivuvyö wasn't the only one who constantly made quips about the knitted truncheons and handcuffs adorning his woolly jumpers.

It was no wonder that Tiilihella was still married, though many police marriages ended in divorce. The only thing more difficult was when both partners were police officers. Rather than allowing the couple to support each other in their stressful jobs, it simply meant neither of them had any escape from the dark side of their work.

Tiilihella glanced at my bulletin board. The cut-out of the angel was now accompanied by Koivuvyö's list of murders or attempted murders committed by women.

'Koivuvyö and Nikulainen have combed through that list. Nothing.'

Tiilihella scratched his beard and sighed.

'Have you got anything else?'

'I still think we should publish extracts of the diary in the newspaper.'

'That matter is closed!' Tiilihella snapped and to underline his words struck his fist against the bulletin board so hard that it shuddered.

The board began swinging back and forth. I was afraid it might fall off the wall, but the swaying slowed until eventually the board came to a halt, slightly askew. The angel cut-out came loose from underneath its pin and floated to the floor.

Tiilihella crouched down and tried to pick it up. His hand stopped midway, and he winced with pain. He pressed a hand against the small of his back; bending over had clearly caused him a twinge of sciatica.

He straightened his back as much as he could with the pain. For a moment, he was like a dying animal that didn't want to let its predators know its weaknesses. But I knew: he had strained his back so badly again that he would have no option but to go on sick leave. I would have to stand in for him.

I left Tiilihella to muster his strength and went to his office to fetch his jacket and briefcase. I helped him up from the chair and assisted him with his jacket. We walked off together, slowly and shuffling—Tiilihella had to lean against me—towards the lifts.

When the lift arrived, he looked around, almost panicked. Luckily there was nobody else in the lobby. He seemed relieved that no one except me and Koivuvyö, who had quickly rushed to help, had witnessed his agony.

In the car park, as if by an unspoken agreement we headed towards Koivuvyö's trusty old Volkswagen. There was no way Tiilihella could drive, and I had to start organizing things regarding my taking over from him, so it was Koivuvyö's job to drive him to the doctor.

Once Koivuvyö had helped Tiilihella into the passenger seat, he turned to me. One look was enough to tell me what he thought of the matter: Tiilihella's sick leave could not have come at a worse time.

I returned to my office, picked up the angel cut-out and attached it to the bulletin board once again. Of all things, this had to happen. First Tiilihella wouldn't let me retire on time, and now his responsibilities would fall on my shoulders. Not even my usual mental exercises could help alleviate my frustration. I felt like shouting in anger but pressed a fist against my mouth instead.

Koivuvyö would have to take even greater responsibility for the serial-killer investigation while I focused on running the department. It was a good job I could trust him in a tight situation, perhaps even more than I trusted myself.

The investigation had stalled like the trams in heavy snow. Koivuvyö had a habit of looking at things from a slightly different angle. Maybe he would come up with something surprising, something I had never even thought of. In this sense, Tiilihella's sick leave could have been a blessing in disguise.

My eyes alighted on the diary. I was certain we would have already received a crucial tip if *Helsinki Today* had published extracts.

I respected Tiilihella, but sometimes his stubbornness really riled me. His not allowing me to publish these extracts might have been nothing more than a question of power—as if we had to fight over who was top dog. At the end of the day, I was Tiilihella's subordinate. But this was about the most important case in both our careers! Now wasn't the time to play silly power games, and Tiilihella of all people should have known that.

Suddenly, an idea came to me, a little late perhaps; I'd always been a bit slow to join the dots. Tiilihella would be on sick leave, and during that time I would be in charge. I could decide how the investigation into the serial killer should proceed.

I looked in the filing cabinet for Arto Haaleajärvi's phone number and called him.

And at that moment—in hindsight, now I'm certain it was right then—everything started to go downhill, irreversibly.

Now there was no going back.

# Ida

I rubbed my lower back. It didn't like me spending so many hours hunched over my computer. Just when I'd stretched and straightened my back, Visalahti passed by, shooting me a meaningful look. It seemed like he was constantly coming up with reasons to go to the kitchen or the store cupboard just so he could walk past my desk.

I thought I'd never agree to the proposition he'd made while we were having a cigarette on the balcony.

'You need to take ownership of your story and write about your experiences. As long as you stay quiet, they'll keep coming after you,' he'd said, and I'd simply shaken my head in disbelief.

'Ida, you need to go back to Pekka Virtanen's summer cottage. Write a column about what kind of emotions returning to the scene of the crime awakens in you,' he'd suggested out there on the balcony.

Despite my objections, Visalahti's suggestion had been gnawing away at the back of my mind. What if I really could make the curse go away by returning to the site of my own misery?

The Bastard would be spending the rest of his life behind bars. He couldn't do anything bad to me any more. But nothing had come of returning to the cottage. And Visalahti wasn't too impressed when I told him I hadn't even been able to open the front door.

He continued on his way to his office.

I picked up my phone.

I knew the text message word for word, but I still had to read it one more time. I had to see the words on the screen. As if that way I could somehow connect with the person who had sent it.

I could no longer withstand the idea that had been trying to force its way into my mind since the moment I'd received the first SMS.

Once I'd read the message again, I decided to check my email. There was a press release from the police in my inbox. I opened it and held my breath.

Last week, the body of an 18-year-old young man had been found near the central railway station. According to the press release, the victim had died of a heroin overdose.

A thought began to form in my mind.

As if I'd been struggling for breath underwater and finally managed to kick my way to the surface.

Until now, I'd only had a hunch.

Now I was dead certain.

# Kerttu

Arto Haaleajärvi's keen eye roved across my office as he tried to commit every last detail to memory. Arto was a reporter to his bones. When I had called him and invited him for a meeting, he had taken the bait without a moment's hesitation. I hadn't told him anything other than that the matter was urgent.

He looked tired, as though he had been sleeping badly for weeks. His skin was pallid, and his eyes bleary. His proud nose and limp cheekbones were badly sunburned. I hoped this didn't mean that he had spent the summer sitting in beer gardens. He had lost weight, but his beer gut was still there.

'How are you?'

It was as though a dark cloud had quickly glided across Arto's face.

I decided to ask the question again, once we had discussed the matter at hand, though I wasn't sure Arto was in any mind to open his heart to me.

'Fine, thanks. You?'

'I'm doing just fine. I need your help. This is a very big case. We have come into possession of a serial killer's diary.'

Arto could not stop laughing.

'This isn't the first of April, you know,' he managed to spit out.

I was so on edge that Arto's chortling annoyed me. He very nearly got the sharp end of my tongue, but luckily, I managed to control myself.

'Jesus—you're serious!'

I picked up the diary and showed Arto its cover. Of course, he knew I couldn't allow him to peruse it by himself because it was evidence in an ongoing investigation.

I explained that I wanted *Helsinki Today* to publish photographs of extracts from the diary and handed him three pages of A4, where I had photocopied the relevant sections.

Arto skim-read through them and quickly packed them in his bag, as if he was afraid I might have second thoughts and rip the papers from his hands.

That would have been my last chance to stop it all.

But I didn't take it.

I had just given him a loaded gun, and in a matter of days it would fire a bullet right into my own heart.

# Ida

A spark caught the shoulder of my polyester shell suit, and the jacket caught fire in an instant. Luckily the zip was open, so I managed to pull it off and throw it to the ground, then stamp out the flames.

My dad had taken me on a camping trip to the Nuuksio national park when I was a child, maybe ten or eleven years old. He'd taught me how to start a fire but made me swear not to tell my mum, who thought children had no business playing with matches.

This time, even after trying to recall my dad's advice, I'd been unable to get the fire started. It had rained a few hours ago, and the ground was still wet, but when the logs finally caught fire, they took me by surprise and flared up, the flames reaching up to my knees.

Droplets of water fell on my head from the spruce branches above. I looked up to the sky. An eagle owl flew majestically overhead.

I took my combat boots, jeans, T-shirt, bra and underpants out of the tote bag and threw them on the bonfire. I'd already got rid of the leather jacket after bumping into Irmeli in the Quill and Parchment when she said she'd seen me leaving the Watering Hole wearing the same jacket.

I tried to warm myself in the glow of the fire. I didn't know whether I was trembling with cold or because burning evidence freaked me out.

What if it was too late for precautions? What if the police were already on my tail? What if they stepped out from the behind the spruces and handcuff me?

I'd taken the metro to Vuosaari, continued on foot to the woods at Uutela and followed the nature trail, then veered in among the trees. Sitting in the woods were two drunken teenage boys, their heads drooping in turn. At around midnight, I hadn't encountered anyone walking in the opposite direction.

The fire was starting to give off an acrid smoke that seemed to curl up from the flames and disappear into the sky. I was worried the teenagers might rouse from their stupor and look for the source of the smell. Smoke got in my eyes and nose, and I started to cough. I put out the fire and examined the clothes I'd been trying to burn. They hadn't properly caught fire and were only blackened on the surface.

I scooped them back into the tote bag, kicked the coals from the fire and put a couple of spruce branches on top of the black ash where the fire had been. Then I returned to the nature trail. I took a different route back so that the boys didn't see me.

At the end of the trail was a large dustbin. Hikers had stuffed it full of empty packaging, so I first had to pull that out of the way. Juice spilled on my trousers from a half-empty carton, and I got ketchup smeared all over my hands, which now looked like they were covered in blood. In a way, they were—that's why I was in the woods in the first place. I shivered and tried not to think about it. Once the dustbin was almost empty, I tied the handles of the tote bag tightly together and pushed it into the bin. Then I gathered up the rubbish from the ground and placed it on top of the bag.

I walked to the bus stop. It was already so late that the metro had stopped running long ago.

I got on a bus heading to the central railway station. The city was quiet.

Suddenly, I got the feeling someone was following me.

I turned and looked behind me.

A figure wearing a black hoodie turned and disappeared down a side street.

I realized I was paranoid. I looked down at my hands; they were still dirty. I took a tissue from my backpack and carefully wiped my hands clean.

Now there was nothing tying me to the Vallila axe murder.

Nor to the body in Hakaniemi.

Nor the Sörnäinen suicide.

Nor the body outside the station.

# Kerttu

'What do I owe you?'

'I think we can call it quits, don't you? You get a scoop; I get to catch a killer.'

Arto nodded and started to take his leave.

'A drink at the Quill and Parchment?'

I politely declined.

Arto had always liked his drink, but his alcohol consumption had started to concern me recently. I remember how, at that very moment, I wondered whether I'd made a mistake. Should I have taken the extracts straight to the editor-in-chief at *Helsinki Today*? Would Arto be able to take care of this properly? Could I still trust his professionalism?

But when Arto said goodbye, his handshake was firm. I hoped he wasn't just putting on an act for my benefit; who knows, maybe he really had given up the booze for good. In the past, he had insinuated that he had considered going to rehab, but what alcoholic hadn't gone to rehab only to hit the bottle twice as hard later on?

Arto and I weren't exactly friends, though we went for a drink together every now and then. We weren't in the habit of discussing private matters. When it came to criminal cases, we had plenty to talk about, and because we were both workaholics, neither of us wanted to discuss anything else.

I didn't know much about Arto's private life. But this was such an important stage in the investigation that I had to ask him directly.

'Is your drinking under control?'

He avoided eye contact.

'You can trust me.'

His word was good enough for me.

Instead, I should have considered how much I was able to trust myself.

I accompanied Arto to the lift, then returned to my office, called Koivuvyö and told him to ask all my subordinates to come into work the next morning. I needed all hands on deck, because I knew that once *Helsinki Today* published the extracts from the serial killer's diary in tomorrow's paper, the phones wouldn't stop ringing.

Tiilihella had been right when he said that all the loonies and crackpots across the country would start calling us. Someone would call hysterical with fear, and demand that the police catch the serial killer without delay. Someone else would claim that their neighbour was the serial killer. Another caller might be so deluded as to confess to the crimes and claim to be our killer.

But I was convinced that, among the flood of callers, there would be someone who was able to deduce the identity of the killer from the handwriting. That was all we needed, and it was well worth all the trouble.

Hours later, Koivuvyö called to me from my office doorway. I looked at the time; it was almost nine p.m. I had been so immersed in my work that I hadn't noticed the time. I realized my stomach was rumbling too.

'Fancy a drink at the Watering Hole?'

I still had a hundred things to attend to, but I was already so tired that I knew I wouldn't be able to make any more progress this evening. Any mistake due to fatigue could be fateful. I had learnt that it was better to leave work until later rather than trying to do it when I was exhausted. It took more time to put out all those little fires than to do the work properly.

I gathered up my belongings and followed Koivuvyö to the lift. He was playing with his Game Boy console and glanced up at me.

'It's going to be a big day tomorrow!'

I nodded. It certainly was! And a busy one too. Thank goodness I knew I could trust Koivuvyö. I didn't know anybody else who was better at working under pressure. If necessary, he turned into a robot and started completing his tasks one after the other like a factory worker at a conveyor belt.

Once things started to calm down, he retreated into his own world and took some distance from his colleagues.

Sometimes I felt as though Koivuvyö's calm exterior was just that, a façade that he maintained to protect me. My job was considerably easier because I didn't have to worry about Koivuvyö's ability to carry out his duties, though as his superior that was most definitely one of my responsibilities. But I was unapologetic about using his way of working to my advantage, and I never mentioned the burden of his workload, not even during our feedback sessions.

We got into Koivuvyö's Volkswagen, then drove to the Watering Hole and managed to park the car nearby. The old place was heaving. Koivuvyö spotted a free table in the corner, and we put our drinks down there. Though I tried to hide it, he could tell how on edge I was. Unlike him, I didn't have nerves of steel. I didn't doubt that I'd made the right decision, but I was worried about how we were going to get through the next few days.

We stayed in the bar until last orders. When closing time finally came and we were about to leave, Koivuvyö, true to form, couldn't resist the slot machine by the door. He had to waste the last pennies he had before we could step out of the already empty bar.

He offered to see me home.

Now I understand that the countdown had already begun.

A week from that moment, and my life would be over.

# Ida

The station wall felt cold as I pressed my palm against it. My dad and I were standing at the very same spot where the young junkie had died. I was certain he'd been murdered, but somehow, I needed to prove it to my dad—naturally, without giving the slightest suggestion that I'd had something to do with it.

I pointed at the wall, explained that the culprit must have shoved the victim into the wall, face-first, so hard that his nose started pouring with blood.

My dad stepped closer. He squinted at the spot, then turned to me, a look of confusion on his face.

'There are no bloodstains on the wall.'

He was right. There wasn't a single drop of blood on the wall. For a moment, I stared ahead in disbelief, before realizing that there was a perfectly simple explanation for this.

We were in the wrong place.

I stepped half a metre away from the corner of the building and resumed examining the wall inch by inch.

Still no stains.

'The cleaners must have wiped it all away.'

My dad shook his head.

'This wall is covered in streaks of mud, graffiti and all kinds of crap. That looks like soot over there! Why would the cleaner have wiped away a bloodstain but left everything else?'

He took a packet of cigarettes from his pocket, lit one and took a nervous drag. I felt sorry for him. It must have been tough being constantly worried about his only daughter.

Had there ever been a stain on the wall?

My breath suddenly felt shallow, and I sensed a knot in my stomach. I gave my arms and legs a shake.

'They did an autopsy on the body. The pathologist was certain this was a heroin overdose.'

It sounded like it would be pointless trying to convince my dad otherwise. It was a marvel he'd even bothered to come here at all.

'Besides, what would a spot of blood prove? He was a junkie; he could have knocked his head against the wall after stumbling around in a drugged-up haze.'

My dad was right, of course. And the police would probably agree with him too.

The police would never find out that this really was a murder. The authorities were happy to believe that another heroin addict had OD'd and died. Just as the police continued to believe that the woman in the bathtub in Sörnäinen had committed suicide and the man found on Hakaniemi Square had fallen and hit his head against the cobblestones by accident.

Maybe I would never be suspected of anything.

Maybe my dad would never have to hear the truth.

My dad turned and started briskly walking back towards the tram stop opposite the station doors. All I could do was follow him.

His thoughts were already elsewhere. He stood at the stop, glanced up at the screen showing the tram timetables, then at his watch. I joined him.

For my dad, looking into five-line stories about the dead was just a macabre pastime. As if he were some kind of Buster Keaton parodying Sherlock Holmes.

He didn't believe me. I don't think he had any idea quite how serious I was. Or that I was serious at all. It was hardly surprising. After all, at first even I had been just playing with the idea that the man in Hakaniemi had in fact been murdered.

A half-empty tram drove past the stop opposite. A ray of sunlight struck one of its windows.

A shadowy figure behind the glass had turned to look at me.

The light blinded me. I closed my eyes. When I opened them again, the tram was gone.

I turned to look at my dad. He was playing Candy Crush on his phone. He hadn't noticed a thing.

Another tram arrived at our stop. We stepped on board and sat down at the back.

I couldn't tell any more whether I was protecting myself or my dad.

If I couldn't do it myself, someone else would have to take responsibility for my crimes.

Suddenly, a terrifying thought consumed me.

I tried to push it away, but I couldn't. The thought throbbed in my mind as though someone had hit a gong in my head.

My dad already knew everything I was trying to tell him.

But he didn't want to admit it.

Neither to himself nor to me.

# Kerttu

Koivuvyö accidentally spilt hot tea over the newspaper, swore, then quickly wiped the puddle away with the flat of his hand. He peered over my shoulder and tried to read it himself, though I was reading it aloud. I had to raise my voice because it was already quarter past seven and the café had just opened. This was the busiest time of morning when everyone was hurrying to fetch a cup of coffee and something to eat.

*Do you recognize the serial killer's handwriting?*

*Helsinki Today* had devoted the whole centre spread to the diary.

Most of the space was taken up with the diary extracts themselves, three in total. This was followed by a short update on the case: the Helsinki constabulary had acquired this diary and was now asking for the public's help in finding the killer. At the end of the article was the phone number for the police hotline which members of the public could call if they recognized the handwriting. Everything was present exactly as Arto had promised.

It felt as though I was able to breathe properly for the first time in weeks. Only now did I fully appreciate how much the case had been weighing down on me. It was as though I had been clenching my hand in a fist from the very first moment I'd heard about the killer, ready to punch him in the face.

'When I get a moment, I'll have to call Arto and thank him.'

Koivuvyö gave a sour scoff. He had never cared for Arto nor for the little agreement we had. Someone might even have thought Koivuvyö's nonchalance a sign of jealousy, but I knew what was really going on.

Koivuvyö knew that Arto and I traded scoops and information about criminals, and he was worried that I was playing with fire. But to date I still hadn't burnt my fingers, and I thought Koivuvyö's concern a little misplaced.

How wrong I was!

We got to work. We had been so drunk the night before that we both knew it would be best not to drive, so we had taken the tram to Pasila.

Koivuvyö must have been nervous too, though nobody would have guessed from his cool exterior. He had prepared everything. We would answer every call, and each one would be analysed in as much detail as possible, though such a procedure would take an inordinate amount of time and effort. Callers who genuinely seemed to know something about the crimes would be forwarded to Nikulainen and Koivuvyö.

We were going to catch this killer, fast. All I had to do was sit at my desk and wait. Nothing could have been easier.

Strange as it sounds, in hindsight I'm pleased that I got to experience at least a moment of unfounded satisfaction. I often think of that day and try to recapture that feeling.

They were the last moments in my life when I didn't hate myself.

# Ida

I stared at the open copy of *Helsinki Today* in disbelief. Why hadn't anybody said anything to me? Everybody in the office knew about it, but nobody had warned me. Did they all assume I must have already heard from someone else?

Wasn't it the police's job to warn me about something like this?

I was in mortal danger!

I started to breathe frantically.

Why was nobody protecting me?

I decided to call my dad. The call went straight to voicemail.

Were these two things linked? The news and my dad's sudden disappearing act?

My dad's phone was always switched on, even in the cinema. He was so used to waiting for the call telling him that I'd died.

He'd abandoned me again.

Just when I needed him more than ever.

# Kerttu

Tiilihella was standing in the corridor with his fingers in his ears, watching as Nikulainen, kitted out in eye and ear protectors, took an angle grinder to my safe and tried to cut the door off. I stopped in the corridor, as if an invisible wall had appeared in front of me and I had walked head-first into it.

I had been sitting at my desk all morning, waiting in vain for the tip that would lead us right to the killer. And I really was just waiting; I was so excited that I couldn't concentrate on anything else. Every half hour, Koivuvyö had popped into my office and given me an update on the calls coming into the hotline, but he had nothing stellar to tell me.

Crank calls, hotheads, nothing but nonsense.

Just as Tiilihella had predicted.

Nothing else.

But despite this, I was still convinced that the crucial tip-off would come in soon.

When the clock had struck twelve, I decided to go for lunch.

When I returned from the canteen, I could hear the wail of the angle grinder from out in the hallway. It grew louder with every step as I neared my office, but I still had no idea what was going on.

How could I ever have guessed?

I wondered where there were renovations going on, until I remembered someone mentioning that the cabinet in the staffroom was going to be fixed during the summer. I was annoyed that nobody had told me when the work was due to start. I hated it when my subordinates didn't keep me up to speed, whether about an ongoing murder investigation or the cabinet in the staffroom.

When Tiilihella noticed me, he waved at Nikulainen to stop what he was doing. It took a moment for him to notice Tiilihella's gesticulations and switch off the machine.

'Damn it, Leppänen! What the hell have you done?'

I didn't understand the question.

I didn't understand anything.

'I did not give you permission to publish extracts from that diary. You have overstepped your authority!'

Nikulainen stood awkwardly between us, wishing he wasn't there. He pretended to stare out of the window, though his bright-red ears revealed that he was following every word of our exchange.

'I didn't need your permission!'

What was wrong with Tiilihella? He knew very well that, as his temporary replacement, I had the same authority as he did. He had no right to breathe down my neck and scrutinize how I did my job.

'Didn't need my permission?' he boomed.

I was suddenly worried he might have a heart attack; he had been suffering from heart problems of late. But I was so furious that I didn't feel a jot of empathy for him.

His yelling pealed along the corridor, but luckily everyone except Nikulainen was busy manning the hotline and couldn't follow the show playing out in my office.

Just then, the safe door came loose and fell to the floor with a clang, as if the power of Tiilihella's roar had dislodged it, rather than the angle grinder.

Tiilihella quickly grabbed the diary. There was nothing else in the safe.

'My office. Now!'

Nikulainen flinched. He quickly hid the angle grinder behind his back, as if to make sure I couldn't snatch it from him. Then he slunk into his own office, avoiding my eyes as he went. He wasn't supposed to have left it in the first place, because his task for today was to follow up on phone calls of particular interest.

I followed Tiilihella in a mood of growing outrage. He had no right telling me what to do.

Tiilihella sat down behind his desk, and I stood opposite him.

'Explain yourself!'

I suddenly felt like laughing, because the situation was so utterly absurd. My boss was sitting at his desk, his face like thunder, though he had no reason to be so angry. I had to hold back my giggles. It was a good thing Tiilihella didn't notice my amusement, as this would have been the final straw.

I told him I had decided to run the investigation in my own way while he was on sick leave—nothing more, nothing less.

My explanation had the desired effect: Tiilihella stared at me in bewilderment. Perhaps the stubborn old sod had finally realized that he had no business bossing me around. He owed me an apology, quickly. I stared back at him defiantly. Eventually, he spoke.

'I have not been on sick leave; I was on business in Turku.'

Tiilihella was struggling to remain calm, as though he was trying to explain the matter to a child or a fool. And that's what I was: a downright fool.

Of course, I'd been aware that Tiilihella was scheduled to travel to Turku for a meeting with the chief of police. He'd wanted to tell him in person that there was a serial killer on the loose in the capital. I had just assumed his sciatica would have prevented him from going.

'Do you really think I would take sick leave in the middle of this investigation? I plan to see this case through, even if it's the death of me.'

He grimaced, as if to prove to me that not even agonizing back pain would make him leave his desk.

'Leppänen, I am hereby putting you on suspension, initially for two weeks.'

Tiilihella's eyes revealed that we were both thinking the same.

This wasn't the first time I'd been suspended.

He had done it once before too.

# Arto

The familiar smell of cinnamon buns felt irresistible the moment I walked into the Coffee Bean. For me, cinnamon buns were like Proust's madeleines. The aroma brought back the events of my past so vividly that I could have been watching a home video.

It was inside these same walls that I'd met my fate: Marja and, years later, Clarissa, whom I'd interviewed for *Helsinki Today*, unaware that she was also Ida's therapist.

Cinnamon buns were a speciality at the Coffee Bean, and their unique recipe was a surprise for anyone eating them for the first time, as these buns had a creamy almond filling hidden inside. The door to the café was open so that the smell would entice passers-by. I didn't need any encouragement; I had a meeting at the Coffee Bean.

To my surprise, the interior of the café hadn't changed, though the four years since my last visit had flown past. The same colourful rag rugs covered the floors, the same pretty lace curtains in the windows, giving the place that special cosy atmosphere. It felt like I'd stepped into my grandmother's house.

I turned to look at the door.

She had arrived.

She still managed to attract the attention of all the other customers as she flicked her blonde curls from one shoulder to the other and started walking towards me, agonizingly slowly.

She ensnared me right away.

Her dress—Chanel, of course—was shamelessly short. What a thought! I realized I was turning into a grumpy old man. Who was I to tell her how long or short her skirt should be?

And with that, before we'd even greeted each other, before her mellifluous hello and my stammered hi, I was ripe for the picking.

Odysseus and I had a lot in common. I couldn't resist the Sirens' call either.

'Arto, long time no see. Thanks for agreeing to meet up.'

I didn't know what she had in mind, but I knew I wouldn't be far off the mark to assume it was something bad.

Despite my befuddlement, I managed to show her I was still a gentleman: I took her jacket, placed it on the back of a chair and pulled it out for her to sit down. It was only once I'd sat down opposite her that I remembered she didn't care for chivalry. I knew this from experience. She was a woman who hung up her own jacket, pulled out her own chair and wrapped men around her little finger.

I'd sworn to myself that I wouldn't fall for her charms a second time, but meeting her after all these years, I realized that such a vow was about as laughable as all my promises to give up the drink.

If she'd wanted to, she could have hypnotized me right here in front of everyone in the café.

I noticed the men sitting at nearby tables glancing at her surreptitiously, but then again, so did the women.

I was embarrassed, because I felt a sense of pride that she was sitting opposite me, of all people. If only these other men knew quite how close we had once been!

Her gestures were subtle, her body language controlled.

She rubbed the tip of her mallow-coloured boot against my velvet trousers. I don't know whether she was doing this on purpose or subconsciously, but either way it felt like being hit by a bolt of lightning.

There had been chemistry between us before, and there still was, though at that time I hadn't wanted to admit it. Now I wanted to admit it even less.

I knew this was the last possible moment to escape. If I stayed here, she would make me her slave once again.

I sat on my hands to control the urge to reach across the table and touch her, to stroke her silken hair, press a hand against her cheek, grip her by the neck and kiss her. But I saw right through her bluff. I knew this was all for show. And yet, there I was, utterly spellbound. She could enchant anyone at all, make them do whatever she desired.

And just then I smelt it. Chanel N°5. The fragrance I'd never been able to resist.

# Ida

That morning, Clarissa had been let out on a two-day release from the psychiatric hospital at Niuvanniemi, *Helsinki Today* reported.

I could hardly believe my eyes. But it was true.

Where was my dad?

All of a sudden, a dreadful thought flashed through my mind.

Was he with Clarissa?

And what if he'd gone into town and Clarissa had snatched him from somewhere it would be easy to find him?

I ran through the list of places that my dad frequented.

The Quill and Parchment? No, then the whole *Helsinki Today* editorial team would have been on her in a flash, trying to photograph her and get an interview.

Just then, I caught the smell of cinnamon buns.

The Coffee Bean, my parents' favourite place. The café where Clarissa and my dad had met for the first time.

I dropped the paper on the kitchen floor and ran to the front door.

# Kerttu

A year had passed since the first time I'd been put on suspension. The body of a pensioner had been found in Helsinki's Central Park. I had been keen to take part in the investigation, because the case resembled one from years earlier: a sadistic murder committed by a man recently released from prison. As the investigation progressed, new details of the case emerged; details so shocking that to this day some of them had never been released to the public.

It had been September. The sky was grey, like a white T-shirt washed with black clothes. Rain was lashing down, and there was a hole in one of my boots. Cold water squelched around my toes with every step. The forest floor was wet and slimy, and every now and then one of my boots sunk into the mud. The only way to free it was to take it off and pull it out with both hands. Though my overall was made of thick material, it too had been soaked through hours ago; so much so that my underwear was glued to my skin like wet maple leaves.

The case had kept me and Nikulainen so busy that we hadn't had time for a coffee break all day. Once we had examined the crime scene, we hurried back to the car. I had asked Nikulainen to drive, but he sat down in the passenger seat.

I rested my head against the steering wheel and closed my eyes. Nikulainen read aloud the notes he had taken in Central Park. I only heard fragments here and there.

I reached for my handbag on the back seat and looked for a painkiller, but the blister pack was empty. I continued rummaging through my bag until I found a crumpled packet of cigarettes at the bottom. There was only one cigarette left, and even that was bent. As soon as I took the first drag, I felt dizzy and nauseous. I threw it out of the window.

The police radio crackled, informing us that a murderer had just escaped from prison and telling all units to go after him. The guy had been convicted of murdering a five-year-old boy only a few months earlier. I had led that investigation too.

The order did not apply to us, only units in the field. I started the car and began driving towards the ring road, where the escapee had been seen driving a stolen car.

'Leppänen, let's go back to the station. The others can take care of this.'

I put my foot down on the accelerator.

When we arrived at the ring road, the radio was still calling all units. We had only been on the ring road for a few moments when I spotted the blue Saab. The registration number was a match.

I sped after the murderer.

I darted in and out between the other vehicles until I got right up beside the car. The murderer saw that a police car was on his tail and sped up. I stayed with him. The rain was heavier now, and the windscreen wipers couldn't keep up. Nikulainen called the station and reported that we had the suspect in our sights. His voice was distracting me, so I asked him to hang up, but he ignored me.

Suddenly, the Saab started swerving from side to side, its tyres skidding on the wet asphalt, until it veered off the road entirely.

Still the killer would not give himself up but fled on foot.

I got out of my car and set off after him. My wet boots felt as though they were filled with concrete. The killer was getting away. Nikulainen was running behind me and shouting something, but I couldn't understand a word.

The escapee tripped on an abandoned tyre and fell to the ground.

I shot him.

I hit him in the shoulder.

I'd been aiming for the head.

# Arto

The Coffee Bean was filled with a familiar hubbub. My head was already a mess, and the noise in the café swirled around me like a surreal carousel. She had utterly captivated my attention.

I wasn't sure how long we'd sat there in an oppressive silence. Had she really lured me all the way here without having anything to say to me?

I sensed that she had something momentous to announce, but she enjoyed keeping me in suspense.

The waiter arrived and cleared away our cups. I noticed that an elderly couple had appeared next to us, smiling awkwardly, apparently keen to sit at our table as the café was full. I helped her put on her jacket and took her arm, then quickly guided her out of the busy café. I was worried she might wrench herself free of my grip, but she didn't resist at all.

I only let go of her once I'd walked her to a quiet side street nearby.

I gripped her by the wrists. The sensation of her body against mine still made me quiver.

I took a step backwards.

'What do you want?'

She looked at her wrists in turn, first the right then the left, and that simple glance made me release them. She massaged her wrists for a moment, patted the dust from her jacket, then adjusted the strap of her handbag on her shoulder.

'This is it. Goodbye, Arto.'

She hurried off towards Mannerheimintie.

I hoped I would never lay eyes on her again.

It was useless.

She had already turned and was walking back towards me.

# Ida

I arrived at the Coffee Bean. I was out of breath, not from the running, but with fear.

Clarissa was dangerous, but my dad wasn't afraid of her. I had to find them.

A woman sitting at the table in the window was trying to soothe her screaming child. At the table next to her, a woman in a trouser suit was talking on the phone. I stopped by a table where a pale-faced teenage boy was slumped. He was so absorbed in the game on his phone that he didn't even notice me.

Clarissa and my dad were nowhere to be seen.

Right then, I realized where I ought to have started my search.

My mum and dad's regular table.

I bounded across the room to the table at the far end.

A grey-haired couple were sitting there. They looked up at me, startled by my sudden appearance. I apologized. Desperation was tying my guts in knots.

The toilets! What if my dad was in the bathroom? I quickly walked across the café, past the counter and along a narrow corridor. There was a queue outside the ladies', but the door to the gents' was ajar. The girls queuing outside the women's toilet exchanged glances as I pushed past them.

The men's toilet was empty.

I got in the queue for the ladies'. Finally, I heard a flush. I noticed I was standing with my legs slightly apart, assuming as firm a stance as possible. I couldn't let Clarissa get past me.

A teenage girl walked out of the cubicle. She and the girls waiting for her headed to the counter to order.

I returned to the front door, hurried to the bus stop and got on the bus.

I'd just sat down when, through the window, I noticed a figure in dark clothes running along the pavement, trying to catch up with the bus and get on at the next stop but not quite making it.

# Kerttu

I retreated into my office like a hunted animal. I didn't want to believe that Tiilihella really was going to suspend me. Again.

I sat at my desk, paralysed, for an hour. Two hours.

My phone rang. It was Koivuvyö. I sputtered inconsolably. Koivuvyö was the only person who could comfort me, but I didn't want him to know that I'd screwed up. Still, I had to tell him what had happened because I didn't want him to hear about my suspension from Tiilihella.

'Kerttu, I'm so sorry!'

It seemed Tiilihella had already told him everything.

I tried to pull myself together. Koivuvyö didn't need me to pour out my emotions, quite apart from the fact that it would have been completely unethical. After all, I was still his superior.

'The suspension will only last for a few weeks. I'll cope.'

'Suspension? What suspension? Kerttu, the serial killer's diary is...'

Koivuvyö's voice sounded distraught.

What had happened?

'You remember that the killer's victim Heikki Kohmalo was a theatre designer by profession?'

Of course I remembered. Kohmalo's home was so stylish that I could have guessed his profession from the interior design alone. In his case, the old saying that the cobbler's children have no shoes did not apply. I recalled particularly admiring a beautiful wall hanging; the same kind that Esko's mother had woven and which used to hang in the kitchen of his childhood home.

'He was in the middle of filming a horror movie. The lead actress Minna Salonen just called me. She saw the news about the serial killer's diary in *Helsinki Today*.'

I couldn't understand why Koivuvyö was so beside himself. Minna Salonen had recognized the killer's handwriting. Perhaps the person we were looking for was one of the other actors. Or someone close to Kohmalo, his partner perhaps. I was right. We were going to catch the killer. With my methods. Soon.

'Kerttu, listen! The diary doesn't belong to the killer.'

A rushing sound filled my ears.

'I mean, there is no serial killer.'

What was this all about?

'Kohmalo made that diary himself. It was meant as a prop, to be used on set.'

My career was over.

But I still had one thing left, something even more precious: my life.

Only a few days later, I would be forced to give that up too.

# Arto

I stood rooted to the spot like a rabbit that has caught the bitter scent of gunpowder from a hunter's shotgun and submits to its fate, freezes, waits for its inevitable death to come. Of course, I should have run away, but I'd lost control of my body.

She had cast a spell on me, and now I was her prisoner.

I felt the smell of Chanel N°5 curling up into my nostrils.

Siiri Hiironen had turned and was standing in front of me again.

I'd cheated on Marja with Siiri when Ida was just a toddler. Marja's perfume—Chanel N°5—meant so many different things to me: love, security, even sex. So, it's no wonder that the familiar scent attracted me like a bee to nectar the minute I'd caught it in the Coffee Bean all those years ago.

I can still remember the way the seductive fragrance had wafted to my nostrils from the table next to my regular spot. I'd been sitting there reading my favourite book—Thomas Pynchon's *Gravity's Rainbow*—for the umpteenth time, perhaps merely to show the other customers in the café how smart I was. I'd looked up, and a woman even more beautiful than Marja had caught my eye.

Back when we got married, Marja knew I'd had a lot of one-night stands before she and I had even met. But she had made the mistake of believing that the vows I'd made in the magistrate's office were forever. And, even more unfathomably, I believed so too. And I might have kept my vows, if I hadn't seen that woman sitting next to me with her come-to-bed eyes.

It was a Sunday morning, but I still hadn't made my way home after a heavy drinking session the night before. I'd spent the night on the couch in a colleague's man cave, and before that I had vague memories of being at the Quill and Parchment.

I must have still been drunk, because I moved over to this temptress's table, gripped her by the wrist, raised it to my nose and sniffed it.

I imagine you already realize that Siiri Hiironen was no shrinking violet. We didn't stay at the Coffee Bean very long before we ordered a taxi and set off to her apartment.

As soon as we climbed out of the pink lace sheets, I told her I was married—too late, of course. She deserved to know this before we had lain down on her firm mattress. Even so, I'd shown her my cards right from the start—or almost the start.

I ought to have realized how serious she was from the way she didn't react when I told her I was married. It was only later that I knew she'd been convinced right from our first meeting that she would be able to break up my marriage.

I wasn't proud of our affair. Especially later on, once I'd realized how dearly I would pay for my mistake.

It was only supposed to be a one-night stand—a one-morning stand, to be precise—and I'd made that clear to her too. But the following Friday, I'd found myself ringing her doorbell in the middle of the night, drunk as a skunk. The next morning, I'd again promised her she'd never see me again, but by the weekend I'd already broken my promise.

I think I must have been drinking out of guilt, though using guilt as an excuse to drink even more only made me feel guiltier still.

It was January that saved me. From a young age, I'd had a habit of doing a 'dry January', and I managed to stick to my principles that year too. As my head had cleared, so had my thoughts: I was married, I had a small child, and I would have to forget about Siiri. And so, after a few months of messing around, I'd called the whole thing off. Everything that had once existed between us was over before it could properly get started.

But Siiri couldn't accept my decision. She started harassing me, calling me all the time. When I didn't answer, she began sending threatening text messages. She even started turning up outside the *Helsinki Today* office in the mornings, waiting for me to arrive at work. At least she left Marja and Ida in peace, or at least Marja never told me that anyone was stalking her.

The few friends I'd confided in suggested I apply for a restraining order. I hadn't had the courage to do it, because I was worried that Marja might find out I had had a bit on the side. Instead, I settled for simply walking past her whenever I saw her waiting at the Quill and Parchment or at our local supermarket.

This went on for years. I'd almost gotten used to the idea that I'd never be able to put my stalker behind me when, out of the blue, everything stopped.

I never found out what had happened, but I'd never bothered trying to find out either. Perhaps Siiri had had another fling and started to stalk my replacement. Or maybe she'd found Mr Right, got married and, as they say, got a life.

Perhaps she had died. I admit that thinking about the latter option gave me the most satisfaction.

I built my whole life around the idea that I'd never have anything to do with her ever again.

So now, several decades later, when I'd received a message from her and she'd actually called me, I couldn't believe she wanted to start the same sick game all over again. Or how easily she'd managed to entice me back into the game.

Over the years, I hadn't been able to erase her from my mind for good. Now, in hindsight, I wonder whether I even had the right to do so. I was responsible for everything that had happened, every bit as much as she was. But we alcoholics never really learn how to take responsibility for anything.

I was still standing on the spot, looking her in the eyes.

She said nothing. I said nothing.

I didn't have time to fully fathom what happened.

Siiri grabbed my head and kissed me passionately.

I don't want to admit it, even to myself, but I responded in kind.

# Ida

The hallway was dark. From the living room I could see the glow of the TV.

I was startled.

My dad was lying on the sofa in an unnatural position, his right arm twisted behind his back. His head was dangling over the edge of the sofa. His left arm was jutting upwards against the back of the sofa.

He was dead.

I took his wrist and checked his pulse, then let his hand slump back to where it was.

He had passed out.

I wondered what to do. Should I try to drag him into bed? I couldn't be bothered. Instead, I threw a quilt over him. He mumbled something but didn't wake up.

As a child, I used to place the quilt over him carefully when he was lying drunk on the sofa. I'd sat up with him all night, waiting while he slept it off.

I took out my phone, opened the *Helsinki Today* app.

Clarissa's day release had been rescinded.

Her holiday plans had caused a storm on social media, and the senior doctor at the facility had eventually yielded to the will of the people.

I'd spent the whole day running around after my dad and trying to protect him from Clarissa, for nothing.

My dad's wallet had fallen to the floor. I took it into his room. The wastebin was full of scrunched-up sheets of paper. He had taken out his old typewriter and started writing.

He had always envied my mum, resented her even. Her books sold so well that my dad and I were still living off the royalties, the translation and film rights. Did he really still think he had it in him to write a bestseller? Maybe he'd drunk himself into a stupor after realizing that his great novel would never materialize after all.

There was still some paper in the typewriter scroll. I tried to resist the temptation, but it was too much. I sat down at my dad's desk and started reading.

The sheet of paper bore only three words:

*My dear daughter*

I took the sheets of paper from the bin and straightened them out. They all had the same line at the top.

*My dear daughter My dear daughter My dear daughter*

The following morning, I awoke to the beep of a text message.

The sender wanted to meet me.

I agreed, though I knew it would be my undoing.

Yes, I already knew it. Even back then.

# Kerttu

No matter how much I try, I can't remember anything else of my conversation with Koivuvyö. He must have tried to calm me down and reassure me that everything would turn out for the best. Empty, meaningless words. Words that he might still have believed to be true.

I went home as soon as I'd hung up and calmed down enough to stop weeping uncontrollably.

At some point, I awoke to the ping of the doorbell. I looked at the time and realized I'd been staring at the bedroom wall for over an hour. I didn't have the energy to get out of bed, but I knew that Koivuvyö wouldn't give up, that he would just keep ringing the doorbell until the neighbours got annoyed.

We sat down at the kitchen table. Koivuvyö seemed lost for words too, though I didn't believe anything could ever make a joker like him genuinely speechless.

He stood up and began making some tea. I was struck by a sense of *jamais vu*, the opposite of *déjà vu*. Watching Koivuvyö make tea felt strange to me, as though I'd never seen anyone do it before.

He found a packet of rooibos, a kettle, the Moomin mugs, spoons and napkins without my help. Once the kettle had boiled, he poured water into the mugs, handed one to me and sat back down at the kitchen table.

We did not say a word.

The cuckoo clock on the kitchen wall marked the hour, then the next. Eventually, Koivuvyö had to leave for his shift. He asked me again, whether I would be all right, and though I assured him again and again that I would be fine, I seemed unable to convince him. He said he would return in the morning, as soon as he got off his shift.

Before leaving, he took a sleeping pill from my medicine cabinet. I swallowed it obediently.

Once he had left, I walked into the bedroom, undressed, pulled on my nightgown and curled up under the duvet. I was certain I would not fall asleep, but when the phone rang at five o'clock in the morning, I woke from a vivid dream.

In my dream, I was standing in front of the *Sistine Madonna* and, where there should have been an angel's face, I saw Esko's instead. All of a sudden, the painting had started to crumble in front of my eyes. The paint flaked onto my face, and when I looked up at it again, the angel had no face at all, neither Esko's nor its own.

Koivuvyö returned a few hours later. My home phone had been ringing non-stop since five o'clock. *Helsinki Today* was hot off the press and readers had read the article telling them the truth about the serial killer's diary.

Koivuvyö realized right away what had happened and tried to unplug the phone altogether, but I fought back. He pushed me against the wall, twisted my arm behind my back and eventually managed to yank the phone's cord from its socket.

People's bitter words still echoed in my ears like the cries of a mob angrily brandishing their pitchforks.

*How did an idiot like that ever become a cop?*

*What a waste of taxpayers' money!*

*Have fun playing P.C. Plod?*

And those were the more polite comments.

I was called everything under the sun and even received death threats.

I had no idea where these callers had got my phone number.

Koivuvyö had come to tell me that Tiilihella had sent him out on a case.

Koivuvyö could choose who he wanted to take with him. Anyone at all, just not me.

But he chose me all the same.

# Arto

I rang the doorbell at the Forest Glen home for the elderly and hoped that the staff would take kindly to me.

Visalahti had told me it was probably best not to warn them of my arrival in advance. I wouldn't be considered a desirable guest; I was there to do some investigative journalism and to interview one of the home's residents.

Initially, I hadn't wanted to avail myself of Visalahti's underhand tricks, but I so badly needed to meet this person, who the editor-in-chief was also very keen for me interview, that I was prepared to renege on my principles. Still, I thought I'd managed to hide from Visalahti that I was there entirely on my own business.

I stood on the step so long that I was beginning to wonder whether I should ring the bell again when a woman with a friendly smile appeared in the doorway. We would soon see whether her smile was as radiant once she'd heard what I wanted.

The beaming lady let me in, introduced herself and told me that she was a carer at the home. Her name went in one ear and out the other, because I was more focused on looking as innocent as possible. Life had dealt me some blows, and it showed. My rough-edged appearance didn't necessarily inspire confidence, but I tried my best.

I told the carer whom I'd come to visit but not that I was

a journalist. Despite Visalahti's cunning plans, I was here in a private capacity, not as a reporter.

Visalahti wanted me to write a piece about the scandal caused by the serial killer's diaries. He wanted Kerttu Leppänen to take full responsibility for the matter and clear *Helsinki Today*'s name.

The carer showed me to Kerttu's room, which was situated directly across the foyer. The room was enough to set off anybody's claustrophobia, though it wasn't cluttered—in fact, the décor was a little too minimalist for my liking. In a most unsettling way, its asceticism reminded me of Ida's room. The narrow bed was accompanied only by a delicate white-painted desk and a dark-blue armchair covered in worn, threadbare velvet upholstery. The bed had been made up with a pretty pink quilt decorated with willowherb.

The window gave a view out onto the woods, which were presumably where the home got its name. The pine trees stood so close together that it seemed as though the building had been dropped from the sky right in among them.

Kerttu had dozed off in the armchair, but when I stopped in the doorway, she roused from her sleep, noticed me and, with difficulty, rose to her feet.

She didn't recognize me.

It was hardly surprising.

We hadn't met since 1995.

# Ida

In the courtyard outside the disused industrial complex, there was no one in sight. I stepped inside. The building was dark. Rain drummed against its sheet-metal roof, which appeared to be leaking. There were large puddles dotted across the floor. I fumbled onwards until my knee struck a sawhorse, making me wince with pain. I kicked an empty pot of paint that was in my way. It hit the wall with a metallic clang.

Eventually, my eyes began to adjust to the darkness. I walked further into the building.

I realized I had stopped in front of a mirror.

My face was red and sweaty. A smile flickered on my lips.

I took a step backwards.

This wasn't my reflection.

This was Mimosa.

My half-sister Mimosa.

# Arto

The first time I'd met Kerttu was at a police press conference just after I'd just started as a reporter at *Helsinki Today*. There had been a homicide, I can't remember exactly which one; I've taken part in dozens of similar events since.

Kerttu had been leading the conference and skilfully avoided all the tricky questions that the reporters present, myself included, shot at her like bullets.

Once the briefing had come to an end, I'd stayed behind and waited for the rest of the press pack to leave the room, then accosted Kerttu and demanded answers to my questions. She later told me that she pitied newbies like me and suggested a deal: she would answer my questions if, in return, I told her everything I knew about the case. It turned out that I knew more than the police did, because I had a source in the criminal underworld who had started singing like a bird.

That's how our collaboration—one could say, our friendship—began, until it suddenly ended seven years later. Only now did I realize that our relationship had been more than just a question of supply and demand. In the past, I'd been unable to admit it to myself, because everything had ended in disaster.

But whatever we called our relationship, the fact was it had come to an end in 1995. At the time, she had given me extracts from a serial killer's diaries, and soon afterwards it had transpired that there was no serial killer after all.

Our relationship broke down. Irmeli Lahjametsä, the then editor of *Helsinki Today*, had agreed to keep me on, even though the incident had badly damaged the paper's reputation. I only got fired years later after turning up for work drunk once too often.

But my continued working relationship with the paper came with one strict condition: I was not allowed to have any contact with Kerttu Leppänen, not even in my free time. The paper's reputation would have suffered even further if readers had learnt that Kerttu and I were still on good terms. I'd promised Irmeli that I wouldn't have anything more to do with Kerttu.

And I hadn't broken that promise, not even when Kerttu had faced a personal tragedy only days after the publication of the serial killer's diaries.

# Ida

It was only a few months ago that I'd met Mimosa for the first time. It was on the same day that an axe murder had taken place in Helsinki, and the police still hadn't caught the perpetrator.

Mimosa had texted me that morning. She told me that Arto was her father and said she wanted to get to know me. At the end of the message, she'd suggested we meet that same day at the Quill and Parchment.

When I arrived, I noticed her sitting at the table in the corner. Or should I say, I noticed that the person sitting at the table in the corner was me? It was quite uncanny how alike we looked. She had inherited almost all her facial features from Arto, just as I had. She too had a long nose, piercing eyes and a pallid complexion.

At the time, I couldn't have said why, but there was something that surprised me even more. Mimosa had been dressed in exactly the same clothes as me.

She was wearing a black leather jacket and a black T-shirt, black jeans and a pair of battered old combat boots. The same uniform I'd been wearing since I was a teenager. And which I'd been wearing at the trial and in all the photographs taken of me.

When we first met, I held out my hand to Mimosa.

'No need to introduce yourself. Everybody knows you.'

I lowered my hand. Shaking hands would have been a very formal way of introducing myself, but Mimosa didn't look like the hugging type.

I sat down opposite her.

Mimosa started peering at the customers sitting at nearby tables, but I didn't know whether it was because she didn't want to be seen with me or precisely because she did.

She got straight to the point.

'Arto cheated on your mum with my mum Siiri when you were only a child. But it didn't last. He ditched my mum after only a few months, threw her away like a used condom.'

Could my dad really be so cold and heartless? Maybe I didn't know him after all.

'Siiri got pregnant. She decided never to tell Arto about me.'

I was sitting there fidgeting with the cocktail umbrella that the previous customer had left on our table, trying to digest what I'd just heard. I'd finally got the sister I'd always wished for. When I was a little girl, I used to dream of having a sister I could play with, race our toy cars, plait each other's hair, conspire together in arguments with our parents.

I'd imagined us playing a game together where we drew pictures on each other's back and the other one had to guess what it was.

Now, obviously, I wanted different things. Someone I could trust, someone I could share things with, someone who understood me.

'You can't tell Dad about me.'

Mimosa slammed her empty beer glass against the table as if to reinforce her words.

My intuition was telling me I shouldn't trust her. What if she'd already told my dad all this before? Or maybe he had found out about her through Siiri?

When I got home that night, I went through my dad's room from floor to ceiling. I turned his chest inside out. I had to find out whether he already knew about this but had decided to hide it from me.

Eventually, I'd agreed to Mimosa's condition. But my reasons were selfish: I was jealous. I didn't want to share my dad.

And later on, when I finally found out the truth about Mimosa, I wanted more than anything to believe that my dad had never found out what kind of child he had brought into the world.

I had no idea that my meeting with Mimosa was only the first stage of the plan she had devised to mess with my head.

# Arto

Kerttu turned, walked to her armchair and took out a board hidden behind the chair. I hadn't seen it before. Attached to the board were a single sheet of A4 and a small picture of an angel.

When I examined the paper more closely, I noticed it had the names of ten women written on it. Each one of them had been crossed out. Most of the names were familiar to me, like the Hakunila Ripper, the Lauttasaari Bomber and the Rastila Poisoner. I recognized the round 'O's, the straight 'I's and the sharp hooks of the 'J's as Kerttu's handwriting.

For years, I'd only felt bitterness and anger towards Kerttu. She had—albeit unintentionally—set a trap for me, one that I had fatefully stumbled into. But now, as she stood in front of me, the intervening years felt somehow empty because I had spent them without her.

I had been carrying two things on my conscience. First, I wanted to apologize to Kerttu for abandoning her when she needed me. But more than that, I wanted to warn her that Visalahti was planning a story about the events from decades ago.

But now, it was too late.

My gaze returned to the shiny picture pinned to the bulletin board.

The angel's face had been scratched out.

Just as my face had been erased from Kerttu's memories.

I could never have imagined the whirlwind of emotions that seeing Kerttu again after all these years would bring up. I didn't want her to see how moved I was. She didn't remember who I was, let alone understand why a complete stranger was choking back tears in her room.

I turned and walked to the lobby, where a nurse was waiting for me. She asked if I had been able to make any contact with Kerttu. I shook my head.

'Dementia has affected her sense of time. She lives in the past. But she remembers the past better than ever. In her mind, she's still working as a police officer, still leading the homicide squad.'

I turned to look back. Kerttu was still standing in front of the bulletin board, tracing the outlines of the angel picture with her finger.

'Kerttu believes she's still investigating that serial-killer case from the 1990s. You know, the one that eventually turned out to be nothing. There was no serial killer after all.'

The nurse clearly had no idea that I had once been caught up in that very same case.

'We use some rather unconventional methods here. I think it's cruel to keep bringing someone with dementia back to the present over and over again. Kerttu's investigations don't harm anyone. In fact, they liven the place up a little.'

I nodded, confused. I saw that Kerttu had taken the picture of the angel off the board and was examining it closely.

Suddenly, a shout came from Kerttu's room:

'Nikulainen! Briefing! Now!'

The nurse winked at me.

'Kerttu thinks I'm one of her former colleagues. I just play along.'

I felt something wet run down my cheeks. I couldn't help it.

Kerttu's tragedy had never left me in peace, though I'd only ever read about it in the paper.

# Ida

Mimosa deftly stepped between the planks and debris scattered on the old factory floor, then waited for me at the door at the far end of the hall. When I had picked my way across the hall in turn, she nodded to me and beckoned me into a room.

It seemed the room had once served as an office, seeing as a sturdy filing cabinet still stood in the corner. Otherwise, the room was full of home appliances. Everything seemed to be broken. A washing machine with its door hanging open, a dented stove, a dishwasher, its trays removed and twisted.

That same evening, after we'd met for the first time, Mimosa had sent me the first of her cryptic text messages. At first, I hadn't understood its full significance. And when I'd received a second message from her in the office canteen, my dad had succeeded in stirring things up by insinuating that this was a message from a secret lover. He really wanted to believe that I'd recovered from my traumas, that I was *normal*.

Once I'd finally understood what Mimosa's texts were about, I thought I must have been mistaken. How I wanted to be mistaken!

I wanted to believe this was all a terrible misunderstanding. I wanted to give her the chance to explain.

And that's why I'd come to meet her again—this time in the cold industrial building where she had been building a rage room.

She'd assumed her role impeccably. After our first meeting, she had managed to suck up my persona and swallow it whole. My way of moving, my facial expressions, all my mannerisms. Even her voice was as thick and dark as mine. She imitated my speech perfectly, its lazy cadence and hesitant pauses. She even had my laugh down to a T.

I remember the way she had observed me when we'd met at the Quill and Parchment for the first time. A lock of hair had come loose from my ponytail, and I'd tucked it behind my ear to keep it from falling across my eyes. She had done the same, though her hair was tied back in such a tight ponytail that not a single hair would have been able to escape.

Mimosa held out a sledgehammer.

'Give it a go!'

I raised the sledgehammer above my shoulders, then brought it crashing down on the top of the washing machine. Mimosa started laughing, and her laugh sounded just like mine. My ears were ringing. A dent appeared in the top of the machine, as though a giant had punched it with an enormous fist. I hoisted the hammer again, gripping its wooden handle even more tightly. This time I aimed at the drum of the clothes dryer. I managed to make a hole that looked like a crater. I dropped the sledgehammer to the floor.

From a shelf, Mimosa took a length of rusty chain, perhaps a metre long, and swung it in the air. It struck the door of a refrigerator. The links of the chain had barely left their mark on the door when she swung it a second time.

She seemed to have forgotten me. Fresh beads of sweat were breaking out on her forehead and her face was more flushed than before. She lashed the door as though it had done something terrible and deserved to be crushed.

All of a sudden, she dropped the chain to the ground.

'I've got news for you,' she said.

She paused. Pleasure flickered across her face.

It was clear she planned to tell me something that would tear me to pieces.

'Clarissa says hi!'

# Ida

Mimosa placed a hand on her hip, shook her imaginary head of curls and giggled. It seemed she knew how to imitate Clarissa perfectly too.

She quickly returned to playing my role. Her posture slumped, and she nervously shifted her weight from one leg to the other.

'How do you know Clarissa?' I asked.

Mimosa began picking at her cuticles. I'd had enough of her caricature.

'We were in the same hospital,' she replied.

The psychiatric hospital at Niuvanniemi.

She told me that Clarissa had been sent to the facility shortly before Mimosa had found herself there too. The first time the two had met, Clarissa was at supper, sitting at an austere table in the further corner of the dining room, alone, staring at the wall, her lips tight and clipped.

'It looked like she was above everything, the noise, the arguments, the terrible food, all that mundane ugliness—as though she was in a different universe.'

Mimosa scoffed.

'Later on, I learned there was a reason why nobody wanted to sit at the same table as her, but no one had warned me, and that's when I made a fateful mistake.'

I knew what she meant. Clarissa could enchant anyone.

The other patients had good reason to keep her at arm's length.

'I can't explain what happened between us. It was as though there was a magnetic field around her, pulling me in.'

Mimosa paused. There was something she wanted to leave unsaid but couldn't. Otherwise, the pieces of the jigsaw wouldn't fit together.

'Straight away, she noticed the bandages tied around my wrist.'

Mimosa hid her hand behind her back—too slowly. I caught a glimpse of the wide scar running across her right wrist.

'Clarissa said it right there and then. She wanted to save me.'

Clarissa had said that to me too. And that's why I'd almost lost my life. No matter what Clarissa said, I knew she didn't have noble intentions this time either.

# Ida

Mimosa was sitting on the washing machine and kicking the door. She was holding a hammer. I was sitting on an upturned fridge. When Mimosa had told me to sit down opposite her, I hadn't dared refuse. I clutched the sledgehammer with both hands.

I was strangely fascinated to note that even Mimosa wasn't immune to Clarissa's devious charms.

'It was the first time I'd felt like there was someone who cared about me. My mum thought I was a mistake, and she wouldn't tell me who my father was. But now I'd found an adoptive mother.'

Mimosa's lips curved into a grotesque smile. I knew I was about to hear something that I would have preferred to shut out altogether.

Mimosa stared at me, hypnotically.

'Clarissa has a secret that nobody knows about. Except me.'

I didn't want to know Clarissa's secrets.

'She once killed a teenage boy. Riku.'

The rush of blood filled my ears.

As a child, I'd given myself a task. I wanted to stop the Bastard from abusing any other children. But Clarissa had committed a crime about which I hadn't the slightest inkling. Not even after sitting opposite her at her surgery week upon week.

'Clarissa's husband Pekka had raped him. Then Riku tried to extort money from Clarissa by threatening to reveal what Pekka had done to him. Can you imagine, Clarissa flew into a panic and pushed him in front of the metro?'

I hadn't prevented Riku's death.

I was responsible for it.

'She managed to stage his death so that it looked like suicide.'

Then, Mimosa told me something that confirmed what I'd already suspected.

Something I didn't want to believe.

Something I'd never be able to escape again.

# Ida

Mimosa battered the oven door, hammering it in time with my thoughts.

Help!

*Bang!*

Help!

*Bang!*

Help!

*Bang!*

Each hammer blow seemed to increase her rage.

Clarissa was still plagued by Riku's death. She was worried that his relatives wouldn't believe that he had died by suicide and might start investigating the matter. His parents, maybe, or his best friend.

Mimosa was speaking faster now. She could hardly wait to tell me everything.

'Right till the very end, I was convinced I wouldn't follow Clarissa's instructions.'

But Clarissa had got inside her head during their 'therapy sessions', as Clarissa had called their shared meals.

Eventually, Mimosa left the oven door in peace. She turned, leant against the oven and looked me up and down, as though she was disappointed that I was no match for her.

Clarissa had assured her this would be a piece of cake.

Staging murders as accidents was easy. Riku's mother was an alcoholic, his father had ended up homeless after Riku's death, and his best friend was a junkie.

I could feel the hairs on my arm standing on end.

Clarissa might just as well have given this task to me instead of Mimosa.

And I'm not sure I would have had the guts to say no to her.

She was convinced that Riku's parents and his friend were the final loose ends that needed to be tied together. After this, she would never be accused of his murder.

But she'd wanted Mimosa to practise a bit first.

The axe murder in Vallila had been merely a test run.

# Ida

The ear-splitting sound of the chainsaw filled the space as Mimosa revved it up to see if it worked. Maybe she planned to dismember my body after killing me. Or maybe she was planning to cut me up while I was still alive.

She switched off the chainsaw and dropped it to the floor.

I was hoping she hadn't noticed that I'd crept towards the door and was leaning against its frame, waiting for the opportunity to flee.

Something about Mimosa's story didn't add up. It was as though she'd told me Clarissa's version of events, but not her own.

'I want to hear what really happened!'

Mimosa's eyes oozed defiance. I responded in kind.

'Fine. I didn't meet Clarissa by chance.'

I waited for her to continue.

'When I turned eighteen, my mum gave me a birthday present: she finally told me who my father was. And she told me I have a half-sister: Ida the Psycho Shrink Survivor.'

If I still had the slightest doubt about what Mimosa was going to tell me next, now it evaporated into thin air.

'I didn't want to approach you without doing my homework. I don't like surprises. I decided to get myself sent to the same hospital as Clarissa. Nobody knows you as well as she does. I wanted her to tell me all there is to know about you.'

Mimosa looked like she was enjoying being able to tell me about her plans. She hadn't been able to tell anyone about them until now.

She had come up with a watertight scheme. The case of the man found dead in the woods near Käpylä had been in the headlines for months.

The crime would finally be solved when Mimosa confessed.

The victim had been in the wrong place at the wrong time.

'After examination, I was deemed *non compos mentis*.'

'How could you be sure you would be sent to the same psychiatric unit as Clarissa?'

My voice was as shrill as a little girl's.

Mimosa laughed.

'How hard is it to cheat in a psychiatric assessment? It's easy—you should know. I went full *One Flew Over the Cuckoo's Nest*.'

'But how did you think you'd ever get out of the hospital?'

'I had Plan A and Plan B, of course. As I said, I don't like surprises. I knew the real murderer would be found sooner or later, and that's exactly what happened. Otherwise, I would have experienced a miracle recovery.'

I knew exactly what she was going to say next.

'That's when you came into the picture.'

# Arto

At first, I didn't dare open the envelope. It was lying on my pillow when I got home late from the Quill and Parchment, where I'd stopped for a drink after my visit to Kerttu.

I'd been waiting for this moment for years, imagining how I would react—as if I could have somehow prepared for it. I'd imagined myself falling to my knees, tearing at my hair and yelling until I was hoarse.

But when I opened the envelope and took out Ida's suicide note, I felt nothing but a flicker of pain as the paper made a tiny cut in my finger.

I didn't understand what I was reading. As if my brain was playing a cruel trick on me and wouldn't tell me what the letter said.

I began reading the letter a second time and let out a burst of incredulous laughter.

Ida hadn't committed suicide. Instead, she wanted me to save her. She wasn't a danger to herself; rather, her life was in imminent danger.

She had written an address on the letter and drawn a map to help me find the abandoned industrial site at Juvanmalmi.

She explicitly forbade me from calling the police.

I supported myself against the wall as I staggered from one room to the next in a panic. It was like trudging through a swamp, and every step felt heavier than the last.

I couldn't find what I was looking for.
We didn't own a gun, a baseball bat, or even a chainsaw.
There was a bread knife on the kitchen table.
It would have to do.

# Ida

Mimosa didn't need to touch me. She just looked me in the eyes, and her gaze told me it was pointless to even think of escaping. I walked obediently from the doorway back into the room.

'Don't think for a minute that the murders were Clarissa's idea! I planned it all myself. But Clarissa really inspired me.'

I'd been right all along—not that it had helped. I was alone with a psychopathic killer in an abandoned factory where nobody would hear my screams.

Mimosa had tied a rope around her waist, and to this she'd attached the hammer. Now she removed the hammer and started throwing it from one hand to the other.

'You do realize how infatuated Clarissa is with you?'

Anxiety made my forehead tingle with sweat. Clarissa probably had all kinds of feelings for me, none of them very positive.

'She used to sit there staring at me with this dreamy look on her face, as though she was seeing someone completely different. And she was!'

Clarissa was not infatuated with me! Of that, I was certain. On the other hand, I'd had no idea she was a murderer either.

'You're her princess, the perfect patient. *The one that got away,* she used to say.'

I chuckled, mostly out of nervousness. Mimosa must be lying.

I truly hoped she was lying.

'Me and her other patients, we were all just substitutes.'

Something strange flickered across Mimosa's face. I didn't know how it was possible, but she was jealous.

'Clarissa saw you in me. That dreamy look of hers made me realize something.'

Mimosa's voice turned hoarse as she continued the story of how she had seen the similarities between us and realized how easy it would be for someone to mistake us for each other. And she explained that turning into me had only required a few little tweaks.

It hadn't even been difficult. Mimosa had been involved with amateur-dramatic groups since she was a child.

'I followed you for months, watching you. Then I turned into you. No—I'm better at being you than you are!'

Mimosa had murdered Riku's father in Hakaniemi, his mother in Sörnäinen, his best friend near the train station.

But these murders had all gone much more smoothly than she had planned. With the exception of the Vallila axe murder, they weren't even considered murders. And the police didn't suspect her of that one either.

Mimosa had no use for me any more.

'But the murder! My first murder, my practice run in Vallila. There was no way I could have known how taking someone's life would affect me.'

Her face lit up, her eyes trained far into the distance, as though she were once again standing in her victim's bedroom, gripping the axe in her hands.

'As soon as I raised the axe above my victim's head and prepared to bring it down on his forehead, I knew I'd found my niche. I was a butterfly that had finally hatched.'

# Kerttu

I gripped the Glock in my hand. The grip felt cool, as though I'd been storing it in the fridge and not in the safe in my hallway. The weapon was light—with an empty chamber, it only weighed 640 grams—but the consequences of carrying it weighed hundreds, thousands of kilos.

It was as though I couldn't get a proper grip on the weapon's polymer frame because the sun was shining, and my hands were damp with sweat.

I felt ill at ease.

I didn't know if I could trust my weapon.

Or myself.

The Glock had been the standard-issue police firearm for a long time, but I was afraid I would never get used to it, that it would always feel unfamiliar, like having the left glove on the right hand.

One magazine carried seventeen bullets. I didn't want to fire a single shot. I had never liked firearms, but naturally I couldn't tell my colleagues this, because I already had to put up with enough comments about how women weren't cut out for big boys' jobs.

This time, Tiilihella had not confiscated my weapon, only my badge. I'm sure this was not an oversight; he probably thought that although I had made a mistake, I hadn't lost my mind enough to go berserk with a gun.

Let alone get involved in the case while I was suspended.

By taking me as his partner, Koivuvyö had put both his own career and mine in jeopardy.

He was certain that we were finally going to catch Kohmalo's killer and clear my name, as well as that of the entire Helsinki constabulary.

The actress Minna Salonen had just called the police hotline for a second time and explained that the film director Mauri Näätä had confessed to Kohmalo's murder at a drunken production party.

And she said that Näätä was currently passed out in bed.

Tiilihella had sent Koivuvyö to arrest the suspect and bring him in to the Pasila police station for interrogation.

Koivuvyö and I had sped to Näätä's home as quickly as we could, cursing every driver who slowed us down.

We were now standing in front of the door to Näätä's detached house. We rang the doorbell, and when he didn't answer, Koivuvyö tried to prise the door open with a crowbar. I'd arrested people countless times in my career, but never with Koivuvyö.

I felt weak, as though I'd come down with sunstroke, I was dizzy and my head was pounding, but I couldn't leave before we had finished. I had to prove to Tiilihella that I could still do my job.

Koivuvyö pulled and yanked, but the door was sturdier than it looked. He swore and continued pulling. I was on edge and tried to hurry him.

Suddenly the door opened, but not because of the crowbar.

Näätä pushed his way out through the doorway.

The killer's demeanour didn't match his name, which meant *pine marten*. He looked more like a bear raised up on its hind legs. In a fist fight, I wouldn't have stood a chance.

But this was not going to be a simple fight. Näätä had a gun.

A Smith & Wesson, popular in the Wild West. Perhaps Näätä thought of himself as Lucky Luke, but his luck had just run out.

He broke into a sprint.

Koivuvyö dropped the crowbar on the porch, pulled out his weapon and bolted after him. It took me a moment to fully understand what had happened. When I finally grasped the situation, I dashed after them.

Näätä rounded the corner of the house and continued running into a nearby woodland, with Koivuvyö only a few steps behind him. The front garden was dominated by a large burnet rose bush, but there were no plants in the back garden; only a vegetable patch that had been left underwatered with dying tomato plants propped up on thin poles. Little by little, I caught up with Koivuvyö until I was almost right behind the pair.

The woodland path was covered in roots pushing out from the earth. I tried to jump over them, but it was difficult; my eyes were stinging with sweat, and I couldn't see properly.

Näätä had pulled further away from Koivuvyö; he was better acquainted with the terrain. Koivuvyö quickened his pace.

Suddenly I tripped on something. I staggered but managed to grab the trunk of a pine tree and, miraculously, stayed upright. A berry picker had left her bucket right in the middle of the path.

Both Näätä and Koivuvyö had disappeared. I continued running along the path. The berry picker, a middle-aged woman, appeared up ahead and shrieked when she saw I was pointing a gun at her. She turned and ran back into the cover of the forest. I kept following the path.

First, I noticed Koivuvyö's blue overalls, which stood out against the green of the woods. Again, I quickened my pace and managed to catch up with him. He had been gaining on Näätä, who was now only a few steps ahead.

The sound of a gunshot pierced the air.

Koivuvyö had shot Näätä.

At least, that's what I thought until I saw that Koivuvyö had fallen to the ground.

From my bullet.

Näätä continued running, and I let him go. I would have let him go, even if I'd known right then that that very evening he was going to get on the boat to Sweden and would never be held responsible for the murder of Heikki Kohmalo.

I cradled Koivuvyö's head, lifted it from the grisly pool of blood and screamed.

Esko tried to say something to me, but I couldn't make out his words.

# Ida

I'd always been certain that I knew what it felt like to kill a person. I've already boasted to you that my murders are works of art! But when Mimosa and I were standing opposite each other in the rage room, suddenly I no longer had any idea how to go about it.

My half-sister and I. Me and my reflection. A reflection of what I'd always feared I was.

A killer!

After the Bastard had sexually abused me, I started to suffer from general anxiety disorder and truly believed that I was responsible for all the violent deaths in Finland committed after my kidnapping.

Well, that's not quite what I believed. Of course, I knew this was just a symptom of my trauma and that I hadn't really killed anybody.

Some people obsessively check to make sure the door is definitely locked. Some check that the oven is definitely switched off. I obsessively thought about murders. Eventually, these compulsive thoughts consumed my mind altogether. I was the most diligent serial killer in the land.

In reality, however, I was a shrinking violet. I would never have had the guts to kill anyone, not even in self-defence.

Mimosa's first message to me read:

*Today you're going to kill.*

When I received that message, I couldn't understand what it was about. I couldn't make out the letters. I rubbed my bleary eyes and moist cheeks and tried again to read it.

In her message, Mimosa was trying to do the same as my illness, trying to gaslight me into believing I was a killer, and she succeeded.

Then, when I read about the Vallila axe murder a few days later, I imagined yet again that I must have been the one who killed the victim. Even though I knew that I'd never even met him. I'd convinced myself that I'd seen myself gripping the axe handle and striking him. It felt like the weapon belonged in my hands.

Then I'd received a second message from Mimosa, when my dad and I were having lunch in the staff canteen. This message said the same thing as the first one. Soon afterwards, the police had sent out a press release about a body found in Hakaniemi Square. The seed of doubt had been planted in my mind.

This victim had died on the same night that Mimosa had predicted that I would kill. This couldn't have been coincidence! On the other hand, who knows how many people died in the city every day? It must have been a coincidence.

But what if it wasn't? I was convinced that the victim must have been murdered. But in my mind, it wasn't Mimosa that I'd seen pushing the homeless man off the bench; it was me.

The third message had arrived just before the Sörnäinen suicide. I had to start believing that there might be some truth to my doubts. Mimosa was the murderer. But I couldn't report her; she was my sister.

It was only when I received the message shortly before the death of the junkie at the station that I finally worked out what was going on.

Mimosa had been trying to frame me for the murders she had committed. I remembered that she'd dressed exactly the way I was dressed at our first meeting. I'd burned my clothes just in case her plans succeeded.

But it wasn't just my clothes that Mimosa was copying. She had held the axe and the Swiss army knife the same way as I'd imagined myself doing it. She had pressed her hand against the homeless man's back and injected drugs into the junkie's veins too.

But I still hadn't contacted the police. I wanted to believe it wasn't true.

And that's why I was standing in the rage room, clenching a sledgehammer, and hoping. Hoping.

Hoping that Mimosa would recant her confession.

# Kerttu

The blood drained from Esko's face, leaving him pale as a ghost. I put an ear against his lips so I could understand the words they were trying to form. His eyelids were pressed shut. I tried to shake him by the shoulders, but he didn't react to my touch.

The weather was calm, but I could feel my hair fluttering in the breeze. I gripped the roots of the pine tree, but we were already floating, rising up until our feet were no longer touching the ground.

I took Esko in my arms and held him tight so he wouldn't fall.

*I hadn't fallen in love with Esko when I'd seen his face in the painting of the Madonna in a Dresden museum all those years ago, but much earlier than that, back when the Koivuvyö family had first moved in next door to us, when I was only six. It was only when I saw Raphael's painting that I finally realized it.*

*Or rather, I didn't realize it in Dresden; I had always known I was in love with Esko, I just hadn't known that I knew.*

We rose higher and higher. I pushed the branches of the pines and spruces aside, so they wouldn't scratch Esko's face as we rose up into the boughs of the trees. We did not stop, and before long the clouds were caressing my face. We floated through the soft, downy filament. I held Esko closer, in order to feel his heartbeat against my chest.

*Suddenly, I caught the sickly smell of glue. Esko handed me a cut-out picture of two angels and gave such a smile that the gaps of his missing milk teeth showed. I took the picture and glued it into my notebook. Then I handed Esko the notebook and he wrote a little rhyme:*

*Every time a flea bites you, think of me.*

*Why wasn't I allowed to love him?*

We were still floating in the air. I looked down through the clouds and saw that I was still sitting on the woodland path. Esko was lying next to me, motionless. I elbowed the clouds to one side in order to see better, but they would not budge.

*It was easier for me to keep Esko at arm's length than my anger, which I was unable to control.*

*I was afraid of myself, afraid that I might harm him.*

*I pushed him away but could not let him go.*

*Esko thought I would change, that his love would change me.*

*He accepted his lot, waited for the day I might let him near me.*

*But more than that, I was afraid of what I would have done to our children. If I wasn't cut out to be a wife, how could I ever become a mother? I never agreed to have children, though this was Esko's most cherished wish.*

*Yet, despite this, he had chosen me, again and again.*

*It was only when I was about to retire that I had agreed to his long-standing wish. We would move in together as soon as I had slammed the door of the Pasila police station behind me once and for all.*

We continued rising up through the air.

Up, up and up.

Esko began to melt. His body was like hot wax, fusing with my own body.

He was me. I was him.

I looked down into the woodland. The berry picker, whom I had startled, had reappeared. It seemed she had witnessed everything and had called for help, because I could see an ambulance approaching in the distance.

The paramedics hurried to Esko's side.

A moment later, their urgency was gone.

I feel myself falling, down, down. I sit on the woodland path and press my hand against Esko's cheek.

Or maybe not. Maybe Esko is no longer in my arms, maybe that too is just a memory.

No, he must be there—right now! I hug him, and my heart is in so much pain that I know that no memory could have had such an effect on me.

It's as though he is still there next to me, fumbling for my hand.

I take his hand, and I will never let it go again.

# Ida

Mimosa picked up the metal chain she'd thrown to the floor. It looked like a fat boa constrictor waiting for the opportunity to crush me. My eyes kept returning to its rusty links. But more than the chain, I should have feared Mimosa herself.

She caught my eye, tightened her grip on the chain. As if for a moment she had imagined I might try and snatch it from her, wrap it around my hands and swing it through the air, even though she knew I didn't have it in me to pick up a weapon.

'Well done, Sherlock! It took you a while, but you finally managed to solve the riddle. I murdered them—every one of them. Who else could it have been? You?'

Mimosa started cackling like a clown in the dream sequence of a bad horror movie. Her laughter echoed around the space as if a whole crowd of people were guffawing.

I realized trying to escape was futile.

'You're the only person who knows about my crimes. You and Clarissa. Clarissa has a pretty good motivation to keep her blood-red lips shut. But I'm a bit worried about you.'

The walls of the room began to inch closer.

Mimosa wrapped the chain around her fingers. Rust flaked off the chain like dried blood from a wound. I turned to look at the room's only window. It was right up by the ceiling. There was no way I could have crawled out through that, even if I'd somehow managed to climb that high. I was sure the window would have bars across it, but I was wrong. Maybe I wasn't hallucinating, wasn't imagining them, because I already knew I was trapped.

'One daughter is enough for Arto. You've had a father for twenty-four years. Don't you think it's my turn now?'

How could I have been so stupid? This wasn't about the victim of the axe murder or the three other kills. It wasn't even about Clarissa.

This was about my dad. I wasn't the only one who was jealous of him.

A look of concentration came over Mimosa's face. As if she were preparing for a demanding feat of athleticism.

I slipped a hand into my jeans' pocket. In my hand, I felt a small wooden doll. My dad and I used to carve them when I was a kid. This doll had a tiny little tie around its neck.

My dad.

My dad was there when I was born. Now he would witness my final moments.

I stroked the doll's necktie. I remember how the wood scrapings used to fly all around the basement as my dad carved little details into the dolls, whistling the theme from *The X Files* as he worked.

Mimosa took out her phone, scrolled through it with a grave look on her face.

'You see, that's me! Birthdays, spring celebrations, graduation parties. Me and my mum, always just the two of us.'

Mimosa shoved her phone in front of my eyes. I couldn't avoid seeing her and her mother at a fast-food restaurant, devouring a Happy Meal at a children's birthday party.

And right then, I knew.

If I wanted to get out of that room—away from the broken appliances and my murderous sister—I had to do it *right now*.

But I was frozen on the spot, like a gangster in an old movie with his feet sunk into a vat of cement. And besides, I knew I wouldn't have made it even if I'd tried. I wouldn't have been able to find an escape route in the dark. At the very latest, Mimosa would have caught me when I crashed into the concrete mixer or tripped over the power saw.

She had already planned how to stage my death so she wouldn't be suspected of the murder.

'Want to know how you're going to die? A street gang dressed in fake Gucci is going to beat you to death when they realize there's no money in your wallet!'

I hoped I would lose consciousness the moment the chain struck my face, and before I heard the bones in my skull shatter.

Mimosa swung the chain through the air without warning.

I didn't have time to react.

I still stood on the spot, spellbound.

The chain rattled against the wall. The clatter of sheet metal was ear-splitting.

'Guess what this chain is going to hit next?'

She stared at me, expressionless.

Of course, I knew the answer.

I turned.

And ran out of the room.

Mimosa was surprised to see me putting up a fight. But I hadn't taken many steps before I heard her dashing after me. The constrictor had turned into a rattlesnake, and now it was following her, scraping against the concrete floor as she ran towards me.

Eventually, she caught up with me, knocked me over. I landed softly in a pile of sawdust.

'Don't even try it!'

It sent a chill down my spine to hear the command given in my own voice. Mimosa was mimicking me again. Was I going to murder myself?

I was still clenching the daddy doll in my hand. My dad didn't deserve a daughter like Mimosa.

I might not have been able to defend myself, but I had to defend my dad, had to fight for him.

With my free hand, I scooped up a handful of moist sawdust and threw it in Mimosa's face. She cursed and wiped her eyes.

And just then, the space was filled with butterflies.

I could hear the flutter of wings. I saw the burst of colour: the Essex skippers, their wings a blaze of burnt orange; the lesser marbled fritillaries, their bright dappled wings gently caressing my cheeks; the grizzled skippers, their black-and-white wings like chequered flags.

'We'll take you to safety now,' they whispered to me.

I got up and started running towards the outer door. The butterflies fluttered ahead of me, showing me the way, their wings beating in time with my steps.

The wind howled as if trying to warn me about something.

I nearly tripped over a log with an axe embedded in it.

I turned around. Mimosa was running towards me.

I yanked the axe out of the log.

She ran straight into it.

Blood splattered everywhere. On my face, in my eyes. I couldn't see a thing.

I opened my eyes.

Mimosa was lying on the ground, blood gushing from her carotid artery as if from a grotesque sprinkler.

# Arto

Someone was pushing me towards a cliff edge. I couldn't see their face. I grabbed the branch of a stunted pine tree. The figure kept pushing me towards certain death. I lost my grip on the branch and tumbled to the bottom of the ravine.

Suddenly I was awake. I didn't know where I was. I looked around. I was lying on the floor by the front door. Ida was pushing me out of the way so she could get in.

She kept repeating one word over and over.

Murder.

I tried to stay awake. I didn't understand what she was trying to tell me.

A drop of blood fell on my wrist.

Only then did I notice that Ida's face was spattered with blood. The shock woke me up in a flash.

The previous night, I'd gone off to save Ida with a bread knife in my hand. I was so drunk that I imagined I was completely sober. I hadn't got any further than the hallway, before I almost passed out. I'd decided to rest a while before going to look for Ida. I sat down on the floor and leant against the wall. Before my eyes had even shut, I'd forgotten why I was holding the knife.

Ida started telling me something about her final meeting with someone called Mimosa, and her voice was so flat that I could almost have believed this was fiction and not fact, if it weren't for the blood spatter on her face constantly bringing me back to reality.

I couldn't understand anything of what she was telling me. According to her, I had another daughter, Mimosa, and this other daughter was a serial killer, and now she was dead.

Ida had killed her.

I still don't really understand it. I'll probably never understand it.

But I've managed to establish some of the facts. Mimosa was a true-crime enthusiast who had become obsessed with Ida's case after her mother Siiri had lied to her, telling her she was in fact Ida's half-sister.

But Mimosa was not my daughter.

Siiri already had a daughter at the time she and I had our affair. I remember Mimosa sitting in her high chair while Siiri and I had breakfast in the kitchen or bouncing in her playpen while we watched television.

I don't think I'll ever believe that Ida murdered Mimosa. It must have been an accident or, at the very least, self-defence. Ida would never have done it on purpose. I'd bet my life on it.

I guess nobody would believe such a thing about their own daughter, whatever the truth of the matter.

Once Ida had told me everything, she asked me to take her to the police station. I suggested she take a shower first, because I couldn't bear to see her bloodstained face any longer. She refused, saying she didn't want to destroy the evidence.

I looked around until I saw the quilt on the sofa in the living room. I took Ida by the shoulder. She struggled, and eventually I wiped her face by force. The blood spread everywhere, as though a toddler had smeared red paint all over Ida's face with their fingers.

I want to tell you something I'd never have the guts to say out loud. But if I demand honesty of Ida, I should demand it of myself too.

With all my being, I'm afraid Ida will be sentenced to life in prison for Mimosa's murder.

But more than that, I'm afraid that I'll never learn the truth.

Even if Ida is sent to prison, that won't convince me that she killed Mimosa.

I'm afraid Ida will confess to a murder she didn't commit. Or did she?

# Ida

I hear the whoosh in my mind over and over, the sound of the axe as I yanked it free from the log.

Can you hear it?

The sound won't leave me in peace.

I killed Mimosa.

It wasn't an accident. It wasn't even self-defence. I wanted her out of the picture. I wanted to keep my dad for myself.

My illness whispers these lies in my ear.

It wants me to believe that I'm a murderer.

When I think of that evening, of the two of us—victim and murderer—alone in that factory, I hear the familiar whoosh of the axe, but in the silver screen of my mind, I see an altogether different image.

I grip the axe, yank it free from the log. Right then, at that very second, Mimosa runs towards me, and the blade strikes her in the neck.

So it *was* an accident.

Wasn't it?

Maybe not.

Now I finally know what it feels like to murder someone.

Or do I?

When my dad wiped Mimosa's blood from my face, I saw a flash of doubt in his eyes. But how do you ask your own daughter something like that?

'*Ida, did you kill Mimosa?*'

The doubt disappeared as quickly as it had appeared. Doesn't he suspect me of anything any more? Or is he just good at hiding his suspicions?

I remember what my dad's eyes looked like at that moment, and that's why I'm certain.

I did kill Mimosa.

If my own dad doesn't trust me, how can I ever trust myself?

# ACKNOWLEDGEMENTS

Thank you to the Arts Promotion Centre Finland and the WSOY Literature Foundation for your generous financial assistance.

Thank you to everyone at my Finnish publisher WSOY, particularly Anna-Riikka. Especially warm thanks to my wonderful editor Irina.

Thank you to Elina Ahlbäck and the whole team at the Ahlbäck Agency. It's thanks to you that *Follow the Butterfly* is currently being read on three continents.

Anu, Kaisa and Susanna: thank you for your invaluable comments!

Thank you, Mark Swan, for the magnificent cover design.

Thank you, Otto Virtanen, for the beautiful author portrait.

Thank you to David Hackston for the brilliant translation.

Special thanks to the whole team at Pushkin Press and particularly Adam Freudenheim for believing in Ida. And a big thank you to my British editor Daniel Seton for your expertise and much needed patience with me.

# AVAILABLE AND COMING SOON
# FROM PUSHKIN VERTIGO

### Jonathan Ames

*You Were Never Really Here*
*A Man Named Doll*
*The Wheel of Doll*

### Simone Campos

*Nothing Can Hurt You Now*

### Zijin Chen

*Bad Kids*

### Maxine Mei-Fung Chung

*The Eighth Girl*

### Candas Jane Dorsey

*The Adventures of Isabel*
*What's the Matter with Mary Jane?*

### Margot Douaihy

*Scorched Grace*

### Joey Hartstone

*The Local*

### Seraina Kobler

*Deep Dark Blue*

### Elizabeth Little

*Pretty as a Picture*

### Jack Lutz

*London in Black*

### Steven Maxwell

*All Was Lost*

### Callum McSorley

*Squeaky Clean*

### Louise Mey

*The Second Woman*

### John Kåre Raake

*The Ice*

### RV Raman

*A Will to Kill*
*Grave Intentions*
*Praying Mantis*

### Paula Rodríguez

*Urgent Matters*

### Nilanjana Roy

*Black River*

### John Vercher

*Three-Fifths*
*After the Lights Go Out*

### Emma Viskic

*Resurrection Bay*
*And Fire Came Down*
*Darkness for Light*
*Those Who Perish*

### Yulia Yakovleva

*Punishment of a Hunter*
*Death of the Red Rider*